Dear Susanna

The book is great, but the sequel 'hero of the mall'

The Road Runner

is even better!

BEN EVANS

Copyright © 2018 Flowerpot Publications ⚓

Cover deign by Becks Neale

All rights reserved.

ISBN-13: 9781980945178

Five hundred men and women in front of a line.

Five hundred men and women pacing, stretching and shaking.

Five hundred men and women trying not to think.

Five hundred men and women staring at a road.

Five hundred men and women beginning to doubt.

Five hundred men and women thinking that everyone is much fitter than they are.

Five hundred men and women wondering why they are here.

Five hundred men and women desperate to start.

Five hundred men and women thinking today may not be their best race.

Five hundred men and women deciding to relax.

Five hundred men and women looking at each other and smiling.

Bang!

Five hundred men and women running faster than they should.

Five hundred men and women trying not to think about how far they have to go.

THE START

I feel sick. I feel faint. I'm breathing heavy, way too heavy.

Why? What's the point? I've walked out of the darkness and I don't like it – it's too bright. Take me back.

Everything makes me nauseous – the crowd, the runners, the legs kicking in front and behind, the cheering, the breathing. It's too close. We're all too close and I can't escape.

My mind was in a safe place. It doesn't want my body to be doing this.

This isn't my world. I want to be in my world.

Take me back.

WARMING UP

The race is the Surrey Half Marathon championship. 13.1 miles starting from the centre of Richmond, running down the Thames to Kingston and finishing back in the village of Ham by Richmond Park. Some of the home counties' finest runners are here, gathered outside a pub on a sunny May morning to compete.

It is a fast course. The route is flat almost all the way, with precious few twists and turns. We will only be running against two things – the clock and ourselves – and as runners, this is the kind of race we dream of. There are some good athletes here and this is why.

I walk up from the Ranelagh Harriers clubhouse to locate the start by the Dysart Arms pub. Some familiar faces jog by.

Cornelius Cooper – Wimbledon Windmilers (Black vest with a white hoop)

Expensive tracksuit. Garmin watch. Head full of thick, blond hair.

Half marathon PB 1.10.48, recorded four years ago in Gosport.

Recently had his second child and lives in a three-bedroom house overlooking Richmond Park.

Cornelius has the perfect life. He went to a great school, earned a PPE degree at Oxford and works as an economist in the city. I don't know why he feels the need to run. Maybe it's because he's succeeded at everything else. Maybe it's because he likes to show how great he is.

'Feeling good today Ben?' he says, slowing up to talk to me. His skin is tanned and he smells of expensive aftershave.

'I'll let you know when I wake up,' I say.

'Yep,' he says. 'Conserving energy Evans, I like it.'

I can't deal with condescension at this time of the morning. 'No point in wasting anything before the race, Cornelius,' I say.

'Quite so,' he says. 'You seem pretty prepared, Evans. Wish I was in quite such good shape.'

He's putting on the pressure, knowing I care too much.

'I'll need to wake up first,' I say. 'We'll see how it goes after that. Maybe a top ten finish, that'd be pretty good going.'

He gives a bored-sounding yawn. 'This isn't much of a priority for me today. More important races on the horizon, but...I'll just take it slow and see what happens.'

'You'll still be breathing down my neck at the end, I guarantee it.'

'I'm not going to let you have it easy, Evans,' he says, brushing back his floppy blond locks. 'You wouldn't want me to let you win, now would you?'

'Certainly not.'

He laughs to himself, a nasal guffaw straight out of the members club. 'I'll give you a head start, how about that?'

'I'll be okay thanks,' I say, stopping to tie my laces. 'Maybe I'll wait for you at the finish.'

Cornelius hasn't run well for a while, but he beat me over the final mile at St Albans two years ago and he's never let me forget it. He's the handsome guy your girlfriend used to date, who she says you don't need to worry about, but who you wouldn't trust with your own grandmother. I feel like he should beat me. He's better at life. He's better at everything.

Patrick Owosu – Belgrave Harriers (Red vest with a yellow hoop)

An ex Ugandan soldier turned British marine, who now works on an IT helpdesk in Farnborough.

Tight, toned muscles. Deep set, bloodshot eyes. Goofy smile.

Half marathon PB 1.12.14.

I feel nervous every time I see him. Each time we race, I beat him – just, but I swear he could run about ten minutes quicker if he wanted. I swear he could kill me with one finger if he wanted.

'Hello Ben,' he says, in deep sub-Saharan tones.

'Hi Patrick.'

We walk towards the portaloos.

'How are you doing?'

Nervous, cold, nauseous, tired – full of Weetabix. 'I'm good,' I say

He gives me his goofy smile. He's missing one of his front teeth and has a scar on his left cheek, that I tell myself he did shaving. 'You going to beat me today, Ben?'

'I don't think so. I'm tired, so I might just treat this as a training run. It's a long way, I'm not sure I've got the stamina.'

He knows this is a lie. 'I think I feel the same way. My legs are like lead weights. Maybe we take it easy this morning and save it for another race?'

'Maybe,' I say.

We reach the queue for the toilets. There's a long queue of women by the cubicles and a short queue of men by the urinals.

'It will be a long day on the battlefield,' he says, jogging over to the short queue. 'You should keep your focus.'

'Yes,' I say.

He turns back and gives a wide grin. 'Don't worry. If you get shot down, I'll make sure someone picks you up.'

I can't help but look at his long, gazelle-like legs and supple upper-body. He is built for running.

Fabien Ward – Herne Hill Harriers (Red and Black hoops)

Current Surrey number one. Half marathon PB 1.09.12.

Clean shaven. Jet black hair. Tall, slim and oozing fitness.

Fabien has won the Sutton 10k and the Dorking 10 mile this season and he will probably win today as well. He's a natural athlete – South East schools champion, British universities champion, top hundred in the London Marathon at the age of twenty-two – but he suffered with a long-term injury a few years back and has never quite regained the form of his youth. He now works as a personal trainer in an exclusive London gym.

I don't want to talk to him, but I do anyway. Maybe it's because I want to be as good as him. Maybe it's because I want his talent.

'Hi Fabien,' I say.

He jogs ahead of me towards the start, head faced forward, legs supple and loose.

'Gonna see if I can keep up with you today.'

He turns and looks back at me. 'Yeah?'

'Well, maybe for the first mile.'

He smiles and stretches out his arms. 'We'll see, won't we.'

I walk behind him for a minute or so, trying to think of something clever to say. 'Are you going for a time, Fabien?'

The straps of his red and black vest curve around his muscular shoulders.

'I'd say so. There wouldn't be much point in running if not, would there?'

'No. Of course not.'

He doesn't want to talk to me. He wants to win and doesn't have time for anyone who doesn't. All I'm doing is embarrassing myself.

I jog off towards the start, thinking about what time I need to go for to beat him.

Dwayne Barratt – Unattached (Orange)

Cyclist, Swimmer, Climber. Maverick.

Sports a blue Mohican, a cut-off orange vest, Bermuda shorts and a range of tribal tattoos.

Half marathon PB 1.08.10.

Superhuman.

'There he is!' he says to me, as we approach the crowds at the start-line. 'My favourite for today – The Guildford Greyhound.'

'Morning Dwayne.'

He has loose, freckled skin, his shoulders are broad and his arms thick with fat and muscle. He looks more like a rugby player than a runner. 'Gonna be a good one today eh?' he says, holding his hand up for a high-five. 'Big time racing.'

'I think so.'

'I just came back from Nepal yesterday, jetlagged to shit. Sat down on the fucking plane for ten hours, not sure I can even remember how to walk.' He gave his thigh a slap. 'Still know how to fucking run though.'

Dwayne is an all-round good guy, with the energy of a thousand pilled-up teenagers and a similarly endless sense of optimism. Unlike the rest of us, he isn't here to race – he's here to run as fast as he can – and if that means that he wins, then so be it.

'At least you're rested,' I say.

'Yeah,' he says. 'Not that there was much resting going on over there, let me tell you.'

I have stopped asking Dwayne where he's been or what he's done. I still like the idea that running a half marathon is an achievement, not just a warm up to a round-the-world cycle trip or a sky-dive off Mount Kenya.

'Are you going for the win today, Ben?' he says, opening a can of Fanta. 'You bloody deserve it, after all this time.'

'I don't know. In my head, I think I can do it, but I'm not sure my body agrees.'

He nods. 'Your mind's writing cheques your body can't cash. I know it well. Maybe stop thinking about it so much, and let your legs do what they're supposed to – you'll save a lot of energy that way.'

'If you do it once, it's easy – right?'

'You bet.' He gives me another high five. 'Don't think about it, just do it. You'll never look back.'

I wish I could think like Dwayne. He doesn't need to run a certain time or finish in a certain position. Some races he just jogs along and talks to people. I wish I didn't care so much.

The start is due to go ahead in ten minutes. Five hundred people are stood outside a pub, trying to control their nerves. They are ready. Their bodies are itching to run, and their minds are focused. They want to go now. Why can't they go?

Limbs are shaken, trainers are re-fastened and last gulps of water are taken.

One more piss, go for one more piss and then I'll be ready.

Nothing will make any difference now.

I'm used to this. It's part of the training, just like sprinting up hills and running laps of the track. I don't need the toilet, I don't need to stretch, and I don't need to drink more water. I need to relax and wait, like I've been for all those other hours of the week. I've done the training, and my body is desperate to run – anything else will only be a distraction.

Don't do it. Let it be. Don't let the desperation take over. It's the worst mistake you can make.

A Bad Start

The Rushmoor 10k, September last year. The course started on a wide, main road, then quickly turned onto a narrow canal towpath. To avoid getting stuck behind the slower runners, a good start was essential.

I was tired. My housemates had come back drunk and watched the entire Star Wars trilogy, oblivious to my nine o'clock race. I was on the start-line yawning, with no teammates and only thoughts – anger, stress, tension – to distract me.

I downed a bottle of Lucozade, then ate some chocolate-covered coffee beans. My heart started to thump. Then the gun went, and I sprinted off the line as fast as I could.

As we turned onto the muddy towpath I was in first place, fifteen meters ahead of Sandy Martin, an ex-track runner who still holds the Farnham Harriers 400m record. I was running like a maniac. No-one went out quicker than Sandy. No-one.

I ran the first mile in 4.43. My 10k PB was 33.20. 4.43 was sub thirty-minute pace.

I was heading for disaster.

It was at mile three that I first felt the energy sap from my legs. I was a long-distance runner, not a sprinter. My muscles had no idea what it was like to run that fast.

We left the towpath and headed onto a main road. The caffeine was wearing off. Sandy glided past me – then another runner, and another. I was going nowhere, not very fast.

With a mile to go, I was still in fourth, somehow keeping a 5.30 mile pace. I hoped that I could stay on the back of Sandy and the rest, then find enough energy for a final sprint to the line. The pain, couldn't get much worse, could it?

It did get worse. The closer we came to the finish, the more my muscles broke down and the slower I became. Runner after runner overtook me. I ran the last mile in nine minutes and finished in sixteenth place. Sandy won by a distance.

Outside the Dysart Arms pub, I make my way through the crowd and find my team captain, Andy, a few rows back from the front. His face is the one I look for at the start of any big race – calm, dopey, aloof, oblivious to all that's around. He will make everything seem okay.

'Ah Ben, there you are. Excellent.' He swigs on a can of Red Bull. 'How you doing?'

'Good, I think. You look like shit.'

Andy is always tired. He works twelve hours a day in a research lab and runs marathons at the weekend. There are black circles permanently under his eyes. 'Yeah, tell me about it,' he says, looking uncertainly at his watch. 'Been constipated all morning. Nightmare.'

Perspective is a wonderful thing. I immediately relax.

Andy takes a tissue out of his shorts and blows his nose. 'I'm not going to do much today, don't worry about me. I wouldn't have come, but we needed four runners for a team, and we've only got you, Dave and Miriam. Everyone else is out on Mark's stag do – priorities, you know?'

'It's the Surrey Championships,' I say. 'How have we only got three runners?'

He looks up to the spectators gathered at the start. It's an audience of three – two old men and a dog. 'Not much glamour here, is there?' he says. 'Most of the guys are saving themselves for the BUPA 10k up in London. At least they'll get an audience there.'

'Yes,' I say. 'But this is a proper race.'

He holds up his hand. 'Let's be honest Ben, this isn't exactly the New York Marathon. You can see why some people aren't really bothered.'

'No, but it's important. You don't get better by racing against a man dressed as Sonic the Hedgehog.'

He pats me on the shoulder. 'I know, I know. That's why you're the man for today. Serious runner. Not bothered by the big occasion. You're the one we're relying on. We're going to need a good performance.' He looks down at his watch. 'Big points. Massive.'

A few rows behind are my other teammates, David and Miriam. It's their first half marathon, so they are full of questions about the start, the course, the weather and how fast they should be taking each mile. They are a married couple and appear happy with their lives. They don't seem to care about who they are racing against.

'I don't like half marathons,' says Miriam. 'You're running a long way, but only completing half of a distance. Doesn't seem worth it, does it?'

David is looking at his phone. 'It's not the easiest race to find information about, is it?' he says. 'They don't even have a route map, let alone details of energy stations.'

'They'll probably have some bananas somewhere on route,' I say.

'Do you think we'll need it?' asks Miriam.

I think of my own nutrition plan – two Murray Mints in my pocket, in case of emergencies. 'You'll probably survive,' I say.

David looks up from his phone. 'I can't even get a signal out here. We're in Greater London for god's sake, what's going on?'

'What do you need your phone for?' I say. 'There'll be signs all over the course, it's not exactly the outback.'

He shakes his head. 'I'm trying to make sure my pacing's correct. I've programmed it in, so that my phone will remind me at each mile marker, then I can slow down if I have to. We can't all just go off maxed out like you Ben.'

Miriam adjusts her watch. 'This will upload to Strava, so we can make sure we've got a record of our times.'

'What the fuck is Strava?' I say.

They both look at me like I've asked them the stupidest question in history.

'If it isn't, on Strava…' says David, in a slow, patronising voice.

'…then it didn't happen,' says Miriam.

'Okay,' I say. 'Whatever. I'll see you at the finish.'

I walk away and stand in the middle of the pack for a few minutes. The smell of sweat and Deep Heat fills my lungs. The pressure starts to return.

The race is all that matters, I think to myself. I have to win.

The club needs me to win. Everyone expects me to win.

I let the tension brew. It's all part of the warm up.

Don't fight it. Let it out on the course. It'll be okay once you're running.

I make my way to the front row of the field. They're all there – Cornelius, Patrick, Fabien and Dwayne. I try and ignore them. As a group, we will be spending the race together, but at the start we are separate individuals, focused on our performance, anonymous amongst the other runners.

There is a clear view of the road ahead. My legs tingle and my arms sting, but I ignore them. In thirty seconds I can escape, and then I will be free.

MILE 1

The shock lasts for fifty seconds. No matter how much I prepare and how many times I have done this, I'm never quite ready for the burst of speed as we push off the line. I am diving into cold water, stepping out in front of an audience, standing naked in front of a new girlfriend. I know. I know what it's like, but that doesn't mean I feel good about it. I just know how to cope, and I know that very soon the pain and exertion will go away. Reacting is wrong, fighting is wrong – my body just needs to adapt and then my mind will be comfortable. Running is all about phases, and success come by how you react to these phases.

The Runner's Journal Entry 1 – Why I Run Fifty Miles a Week

'Why do you do it?' my friends ask me. 'Why do you get out there and run every day? Don't you think you might be a bit of a masochist?'

Little do they realise that in that statement, they touch upon exactly the reason why I run fifty miles a week, fifty-two weeks of the year. I do it because it hurts.

When I started five years ago, the idea was simple.

'I want to run to get fit,' I said to myself. 'I want to lose weight, I want to challenge myself.'

I knew that running was going to cause me pain, and in the back of my mind I wanted it to. In hurting, running validated itself. It gave itself a meaning.

Soon I was running every other day. As the steps got harder and the sweat began to build, the voice in my head said:

'I am getting stronger, I am getting fitter. I am losing fat from my stomach.'

Then, as I started to push through the pain barrier, the reminder became self-congratulatory:

'I have hurt. Other people don't like hurting. I am better than other people.'

And finally, when I ran again the next day, this escalated to:

'I am hurting again, I am getting even fitter and I am losing more weight. I am an exceptional person.'

After a few more weeks, I became fitter. I went from running a couple of miles around the block, to a six or seven mile run around the park. It took much longer for the pain to come. Sometimes it became difficult to find it at all.

'I'm running the same distance, but I can't run any faster,' I said to myself. 'There is no pain to overcome. Where is the pain? I want it back. I want to feel like a better person. I need to keep challenging myself.'

The hurt had touched something in me, it had given me an insight into something different, a better form of life, and I didn't want to leave that behind. Running was now not just a means to a physical end, but an exploration of my inner self. I wanted to see how much further I could go and who I could be in this new, fit body of mine. I wanted to test it further, run that extra mile, see how far I could go until I quit. It was a quest for completeness, to work out exactly how far my limits were.

I started running further — ten, twelve, sixteen miles — and running faster — seven-minute miles, six-minute miles, five and a half minute miles. It hurt more and more, but the sense of achievement grew greater every time.

'Look what I can do. Look what I've had inside me all this time. How much further can I take it?'

I entered a half marathon and finished in the top hundred; I ran a 10k in thirty-six minutes; I won the local 5k time trial.

'This is incredible. I've never won anything. What else can I do?'

Then, after three ten-mile runs in a row, I started to find my boundaries. Whenever I thought about the day ahead, I dreaded the experience of running. I ran into tiredness now, but nothing more, just aches, twinges, pain and endless, endless fatigue. There was nothing else. I couldn't push through.

'That's it,' I said. *'That's all I can take. I'm done.'*

But a few days later, for some reason, I found that I could keep going. I went out on a cold Sunday morning, and ran laps and laps of the park, forcing myself forward, feeling like dying, feeling like I could do no more, then somehow kept going, and going, and going, and ran further than I ever had before. The whole world around me began to change. I'd crossed onto a new plain. Nothing hurt anymore. I wasn't tired. I could keep going forever and never have to stop!

From the physical to the mental, running had now entered the realm of the spiritual — it had taken me from somewhere plain to somewhere amazing, a place where very few are able to go. After this day I found that my boundaries were much further than I realized. I could run a marathon. I could win a marathon. I could go to Boston and run with the elite.

The feeling didn't last forever, but the memories have, and I hold them with me to *this day. This is why I run as I do. I know that somewhere in this first step, when my breath begins to falter and my foot starts to ache, there lies somewhere in me a feeling more alive, more fantastic than anything I have ever felt, and the more the pain increases, the greater it will be when I run through it. On the other side is something truly incredible.*

This is the reason why I run. This is where running can take me.

The first minute of the race passes without drama. All the tension of the start ebbs away, and I relax into my comfortable stride. Around me other runners are gasping for breath – teeth gritting and arms flailing. They've gone off too fast, thinking that they might be able to chase us down. They don't realize yet who they are, how average they are and how ten weeks of training does not turn you into a professional.

They were me. They still are me much of the time, but not today. For this race I am at the front, I am a leader and I am doing things right. I try to ignore them so I can remember this – that I am in my rightful place and that they are no longer a part of me.

Fabien and Dwayne are also beginning to relax, cutting through amateur limbs like smiling assassins. I can't hear them breathing, but I recognise them by the rhythm of their strides. Dwayne is loose and languid, Fabien is measured and perfected. They are both artists – Jackson Pollock and Raphael, Punk and Puccini – beautiful in their own ways. I try to block them out and focus on my own race, but no matter how much I try I cannot ignore the movement of their bodies. It sits in the back of my head for the whole thirteen miles, like an itch that I just can't reach.

Right – down, right – up, left – down, left – up, quad, knee, calve, foot, quad, knee, calve, foot – over and over, mile after mile.

Imagine sitting in a room with a ticking clock – tick, tock, tick, tock – over and over, for an hour, when suddenly there is a tock, TOCK. All of us are waiting for a tock. That is when we strike.

The route leads us breathlessly into Richmond – coffee shops, dog-walkers, Range Rovers, the Thames – and the pack flows behind, removing the slower sediment who see the comforts of Boots, John Lewis and Starbucks and remember the reality that they have left. A few minutes was enough. Lungs hurt and chests ache. They can't keep this up – six minutes a mile. It's time to drop back.

It's fine for them. They shop at Waitrose and eat at restaurants on Saturday night. They have normal lives. It isn't possible for them to embrace suffering, like Dwayne, Fabien or me. There is nothing wrong with how they feel. It takes a lot to reach beyond this. Waitrose is a good shop. It won't turn you into a superman, but it sells some quality products. That's important. That's why people shop there. How can you be that person who goes somewhere else?

The race is all that matters to me. Elite athletes must be in a different place, where Starbucks, Facebook and Waitrose are not important. Their lives shouldn't revolve around a pub or a coffee house, or going out for dinner, or shopping at B&Q on a Sunday. They shouldn't need to buy a new outfit for this or have a new gadget for that. The food they eat should be plain and energy-boosting. They need to run and then run again, and then work up to the big run at the weekend. The rest of this – consumer life – should be a distraction, an irritation and then a relic. It's all time when they could be running, or resting so that they can run again. It's a waste, a trash dump for the normal people. Let them enjoy it.

I am in this zone. I am running at the 5.20 mile pace that I aim to maintain for the rest of the race. I am relaxed and feel that I should have no problems maintaining this. The spring sales will not convince me otherwise.

We rumble up to Richmond Bridge. It is a small incline, no more than twenty feet, but is enough to ensure that the last of the hopeful few have dropped back into anonymity – fiftieth, twenty-ninth, sixty-fifth – positions that will mean nothing to anyone apart from them. Fabien leads us off, as is the given for the man in form, and I sit behind Dwayne in third. Behind me, I can feel Cornelius striding. I may not be able to see him, but his form is in my head. Three years of racing. The experienced runner has eyes in the back of his head.

Over and down. A brief glimpse of the Thames before a long descent into suburbia.

Long roads now. Tall stone houses break the breeze from the water. A car, a bike, a man walking his dog. People enjoying the comforts of success. They don't like us. We are intruders, spreading pain and determination into their world.

Fabien is ahead, five meters down the road, Cornelius has moved up alongside me and Patrick is sat behind, panting like he's hungry for a kill. No-one wants to make a move. Get the first mile done; make sure we are all on target and make sure the pace is right.

Nothing is certain until the stopwatch is checked. The human mind is not a ticking clock. Once we find it, we can maintain an almost perfect rhythm, but finding the right rhythm is not simple. We must remove everything else – tension, lethargy, comfort, distractions – and revert to our practiced pace. This will happen naturally once fatigue sets in, because we will simply be unable to run any faster, but as serious runners we need to be at this level from the start. If we are running too hard or too slow, we will not win. Fabien knows this, Patrick knows this, Cornelius knows this – even Dwayne knows this. We need the certainty of that first mile marker. Until then, we are looking to each other for the right speed, a herd without a bull to lead us. Cowards, but cowards with a good reason for being so.

The mile marker approaches we take a swift glance at our watches.

5.13.

That's good. A bit too fast, but it's always like that. It wouldn't be a race if the first mile wasn't fast.

For the moment I'm happy. Mile 2 is happy time.

MILE 2

The road leaves Richmond and meanders slowly downhill toward the Thames. The river runs alongside, slipping and slopping a few metres below. It's soothing to my limbs.

  I begin to relax. The noise of the town abates. Blood filters into my legs, causing my brain to slow down. I'm still aware of my surroundings, but I can only process thoughts in simple ways – a house, a tree, a car. There's no point in wasting energy when the body is trying to survive.

  I knew this was coming and I was looking forward to it. It's when running becomes a therapeutic experience.

The Runner's Journal Entry 2 – Running to Simplicity

Running is a simple activity. It doesn't take a modern, highly evolved brain to tell you how to do it, in fact there is no point thinking about it because it doesn't take any thought. You just have to put one foot in front of the other. One foot, next foot, one foot, next foot, nothing more. What could be easier?

On a particularly long run, I don't have any thoughts at all. The blood has drained from my head into my legs, and my brain has become a pile of thoughtless mush. Simple ideas are as complex as advanced algebra. Old worries or desires are meaningless. I have no choice but to think about nothing, and it is in that mindset that running becomes perfect. There are no thoughts or worries. All you have to do is run. It is the simplest act in the world.

Yet, in our modern lives, we don't find much time for simple activities. Our minds are used to more complex and exciting sensations – fast cars, busy shops, instant news, social media. The idea of silence and stillness seems to belong to a very different age. It is therefore strange that in such sophisticated place, we have found so much room for running. Why do we do it? What is it about us that finds such pleasure in this rather mundane activity?

The simple answer, I think, is because we are human beings.

The modern world is a place full of excitement, entertainment and pleasure, and in many ways it's a really cool place to live. We are wealthier, more tolerant, healthier and more sophisticated than we ever have been before. We are trying to find better ways to live together and share the world amongst us. We are trying to make a better future. However, in this land of sophistication and tolerance we occasionally forget one important thing. We are humans. We have basic, underlying needs. Our DNA is still not far removed from that of a gorilla.

Prehistorically, we would express our primitive nature in acts such as grunting, fighting and shagging, and of course we still do, but in the modern world we are looking for more sophisticated outlets. There are many solutions to this — shouting at footballers, getting raucously drunk, going to strip clubs, lifting weights, Zumba classes — and they are important for us to have. We either let out our primitive urges or suck them in, but deal with them we must, and the best way I think to do this, is through running. There is no cost — social or financial — there is no hurt to others and afterwards there is no hangover to deal with. By doing it, we are performing a primitive action, not replacing it with something else, and so it feels more authentic than any of the equivalents. There is nothing quite like the real thing after all.

Running is important in our new world because it is the very opposite of everything that has made it non-human. It is a reminder of what lies behind the flashing lights, the mobile screens, the roaring motorways and the busy high streets. It brings us back to what we are as human beings, in all our glory and all our shortcomings. It is what is real, and reality makes us happy. That is why all the problems of the day seem to flow out of us after a run in the evening — we can take a step back, remember what we really are and consider what is important and what isn't. Other mediums may claim to do the same thing — socializing, movies, television — but all they are doing is replacing one distraction with another. If our basis for reality is drinking, Facebook or EastEnders then we have a problem; but running is something that is real.

The simplicity of running therefore provides a perfect way of clearing the clutter that builds up in our crowded lives. It does not replace it — we could not run all the time after all — but it helps us insert our living, breathing, Homosapien selves back into it. It is important that we keep it this way.

As if threatened by this simplicity, the modern world is trying to drag running out of its primitive utopia and into its synthetic clutches. No longer is it a thing of simple beauty, running is now a 'lifestyle', a fashion and a statement of who you are as a person, and in turn it requires a uniform, a posture and a set of accessories. Running has become cool, and cool is not simple. Now when we run we are not being ourselves, rather we are figures drawn from an idea in a meeting room, and this is not what it should be about. Reject it! Throw off your I-Phone and its playlist, your water bottle and your sweatband, your energy patches and your Runners World, even your stopwatch, and run for the pleasure of it, of putting one foot in front of the other.

It will remind you why you are doing it in the first place. It will remind you what it is to be human.

On the road, I catch a glance of the Thames. Sunlight glints from the ripple and flow of the water, and swans float gracefully over the surface. I inhale a deep breath of the crisp morning air. Easy. This race is easy. Maybe I can go quicker? Maybe I am better than I think?

I pass Cornelius, and up the pace towards Fabien. He is around ten meters ahead. This might not seem like much, but it can be staggeringly difficult to close down if left for too long. The distance of the half marathon deludes you into believing that letting an opponent move away is not a serious problem, but it is. We will be running this race at about a mile every five-and-a-half minutes. That's about five metres a second. If I let someone escape to fifty or sixty metres in front of me, I'll have to run ten seconds faster to catch him up within a mile. This is a serious change in pace and could lead to me burning out later in the race.

Instead, I'll need to make the distance up gradually over three or four miles, then hope that Fabien doesn't have any more in the tank. It'll be difficult to do. Fabien is no amateur – he'll know that I'm coming – but if I delude myself otherwise, then I'm not thinking in terms of endurance running, I'm back in the other world, back in Richmond, where people can just go faster and where there is always a quick fix. The race is not like this. Small choices can lead to great problems. That's why I won't let Fabien get away any further, and why Patrick, Cornelius and Dwayne won't let me get more than ten metres ahead of them. It's a game that will continue for the next twelve miles.

My extra kick of speed has shaved off a second or so, and it is enough to take me behind Fabien's red and black vest. The others are making sure we don't go any further away, keeping us within an invisible band, but also not catching us. I try to concentrate on Fabien to take me forward. His club colors repel me like a raging wasp – dark, blood and hell – but his running style is fluid and confident, and it is easy to match his rhythm. My legs follow his. I stick out my chest. His ego becomes mine.

I'll eventually be too tired to keep this pace alone, so I need these moments of parasitic running to save on energy. Digging deep will become easier if I can keep my reserves as full as possible. Fabien is a winner, and if I can ape a winner then I will be okay.

A kilometre passes without another thought. I have lost myself for over three minutes and the mile is almost over. Was I running fast or slow, good or bad? I don't know. My mind's been elsewhere. I've been running on autopilot, guided by Fabien. At some point he's turned off the road and is haring down a narrow path towards the Thames. Is this the right way?

I am a coward, right? Sitting in the tow of another athlete, running his run, thinking his thoughts, keeping his pace. I'm not racing. I am following like a dog. Fabien should run alone without a Siamese twin feeding off him. Where are you? Where is the individual? Where is Ben from Guildford and Godalming? Why doesn't he step out on his own for once?

This is how running works I'm afraid. It's the same all the way down, from second to four hundred and ninety-second. We all do the same thing – follow the leader. I wish it wasn't this way. I wish I could just run much faster than everyone else, but it doesn't work like that. Unless you're Paula Radcliffe or Emil Zatopek, you're only ever going to be slightly better than anyone else, and so you have to use everything you can to be first over the line. I'm saving energy by following Fabien. A few meters back Dwayne, Cornelius and Patrick are doing the same to me. We all use each other because it means we can run faster. None of us are Paula Radcliffe or Emil Zatopek. Having an ego in running is all very well, but you need to be good. Only a special person can beat the half marathon alone...although he is probably wearing a red and black vest.

5.11. Fabien is very consistent.

MILE 3

A look at the watch and my ego returns with a vengeance. My time following Fabien made me feel good – calm, slick and calculated – but the goodness has gone. Ben is back, and he wants to re-assert his authority.

Why are you doing this? he says to me.

Stop hurting yourself.

You won't win. You don't want to win.

You're not the competitive type. You hate people like this.

You're far too tired, too tired, too tired.

The route zig-zags under bridges, dances along cobbles and opens out onto the Thames Path. There are couples walking dogs, tramps sleeping on benches and families cycling lackadaisically. I can hear them thinking as I pass:

What a beautiful morning.

Who are these runners?

Why do they hate themselves so much?

I can feel my pre-running self, sitting outside my body and shaking his head. Why are you doing this to yourself?

The Runner's Journal Entry 3 – Reasons not to Run

How wonderful it is to be a runner. How fabulous we feel, breathing in the fresh air of a sunny Sunday morning, working our taught legs and expanding our capacious lungs, feeling fit and happy with the world. What pleasure we attain. How blessed we are to follow this path.

This is why we do it, and this is why we wonder why everyone else doesn't do it too. Running makes you feel fantastic. Who would not want to take it up right now?

And yet most of my friends don't run. In fact, almost no-one I know does. So why? If running is such an innate human capability and so ultimately pleasure-inducing, why doesn't everyone do it? Why was it only me, a seventy-year-old man with a beard and a chubby Chinese woman with headphones, out in the park this morning?

Reason 1: Lethargy

The human body operates on momentum. Left to its own devices it will happily sit on the couch and do nothing for most of the day. We are programmed to save energy for hunting or running away from danger, so we see unnecessary exertion as a bad thing. Most days we resemble a stubborn old carthorse, shaking its mane and stamping its hooves at any unnecessary levels of work:

'Why?' we groan, dragged out for a short jog. 'What are you doing? Stop it, stop it now! I'm not running, I have to rest. Let me rest.'

The muscles tense up and send defamatory messages to the brain. Mucus forms over the throat. Carbon dioxide builds in the stomach. Lactic acid stings the joints. Running feels dreadful. It is torture.

It is not long before we return to the sofa, turn on the TV and relax.

'Fuck that,' we think. 'It's not worth it.'

And we never go running again. The body is much happier to wait in its lethargic cocoon. It is what takeaway pizza was made for.

Reason 2: Embarrassment

In our heart of hearts we know that running is good for us. We know it will make us look better, feel better, and every morning we look outside and think about doing it, but then something stops us, something says that maybe it would be better to stay inside and do it another day.

I'll look stupid.

People will laugh at me.

I'll be so slow.

I don't know what to wear.

Everyone will stop and stare.

Someone I know might be there.

Running is a very individual pursuit. This is fantastic in many ways, but is not helpful when it comes to starting in the first place. No one can tell you to run. You can't go and have a run-about with your mates. If you want to run you have to do it on your own, with only your self-consciousness for company, and we don't tend to like things that make us feel like this.

Another simple fact is that the actual act of running is not particularly cool. You certainly do not look good when you are doing it and the idea of the general public eyeing your sweaty body lolloping around the park is a pretty excruciating concept to deal with alone. Essentially you are shouting to the world:

'Look at me! Look at how unfit I am. Look how hard I need to try to work off this fat. What a pathetic hopeless loser.'

It is much better to stay indoors and not run at all.

Reason 3: Boredom

It's a hard sell to a non-runner:

'I'm off for a run. I'm going ten times round the park for about two hours. Hopefully the rain will stop and the frost will thaw out a bit.'

Why? Why on earth would anyone do this out of choice? It doesn't matter how fit it might make you – it's an awful way to spend your time.

The simple fact is that, taken on its own, running is very boring. One foot after another, over and over, round and round, legs getting more tired and the road getting longer and longer. There is no ball to catch, no net to shoot into, no tackle to make – it is dull, monotonous and exhausting.

To the mind of the modern person, this is an unpalatable concept. We don't like being bored. In a multimedia world we don't know how to be. If there is a TV in the room, we turn it on. We don't sit in silence, listening to our breaths. However, this is exactly the situation we are placing ourselves into when we run. We are choosing to be alone with our thoughts, and these thoughts are mainly concerned with how much we hate what we are doing. It doesn't make sense, particularly when there are so many more interesting things out there. What time does Holby City start?

Reason 4: Runners are self-satisfied pricks

Oh God. Oh God look at them. Look at their tanned legs, their Lycra tops, the smug smiles over their chiselled faces. What are they so happy about? How can they be that pleased with themselves?

No-one wants to turn into these people. Any of us who retain a shred of integrity and self-worth do not see these robots as figures to aspire to. We may not have their gorgeous bodies and great tans, but at least we can talk about more than how wonderfully fit we are. When we go down the pub, we can have a laugh instead of sipping on lemonade, going home at ten and making everyone else feel guilty about their lives.

This is a problem with sport, and with running in particular. It starts in school, when the athletes tend to be brainless jocks; moves on to university, where they are viewed as antisocial freaks; and then to adult life, where they appear far too self-content to be likeable. Footballers may be dumb, but they are popular; rugby players are loud and boorish, but a great laugh down the pub; and bodybuilders can at least be a good help in a late-night dust-up. However, runners are none of these things. They are either smug and fit, or weird and introverted, and are therefore not the kind of people you want to hang around with. Social ineptitude is, you suspect, one of the reasons they became runners in the first place.

No, running turns you into a sexless, personality-less automaton – Barbie or Ken – with a brain pumped full of endorphins and not much else, and for that reason I'll stay in on a Sunday morning thanks very much.

So there it is. Four damn good reasons why a considerable majority of the population chooses not to adopt the wonderful pursuit of long distance running. It's hard, it's embarrassing, it's dull and it turns you into a risible human being.

However, when you consider running for what it truly is, you realise that none of this is really true. Yes, I may not always enjoy going out for a ten-mile hill session on a Sunday morning, but each time it gets easier, each time it hurts less and each time I realise that I am improving that little bit. Yes, I run laps around the park, but I am doing it for a reason – to get quicker, to make that six-minute mile pace, to sprint the whole of the big hill at the end, to win that half marathon in three months' time – so I can celebrate with all my friends from the club who aren't the self-important twats I thought they might be. That is when the pain becomes worthwhile. That is when I am quite the opposite of shy and embarrassed. That is when you can enjoy a good night out, knowing that you have achieved something.

It is always easy to find reasons not to do things, but then you'll never know what you can do. Get out, push those boundaries and don't worry about what other people think. It will make your life much more interesting.

'Come on! Keep going!' shouts a marshall from under the bridge. 'You can do it!'

Dwayne has overtaken me, Patrick has overtaken me, and Fabien has stretched his lead to around fifteen metres. Only Cornelius is behind me because he likes to pose for the female marshals. He'll be ahead of me soon, it's only a matter of time.

I've lost focus. My body can't do everything on its own, it needs the mind to drive it forward. Descartes was obviously not much of a runner. Whatever his reason may have told him, the body and the mind cannot exist separately. Only when the two are in harmony are you able to race properly. Without the mind, the legs will run until they're tired, but they won't go any further. With the mind, you can push them through the pain and the fatigue, to a place where they can move faster and further. In a race you must exist at this threshold because otherwise you will not be able to stay at the front. It must be a constant 110%. 'The zone.'

We all have our individual ways of taking our bodies to this place of peak performance. It's what makes us the unique runner we are:

Cornelius:

The running entrepreneur. He is late to the sport, but he has succeeded at everything else in life – education, employment, marriage, kids – so he will succeed at this as well. He focuses on one thing obsessively, then lives in that zone for as long as it takes to perfect it. At the moment this zone is running. He doesn't win all the time, but he knows that second or third place is just a step on the inevitable path to first.

Unfortunately, running needs more than this. It makes you so fragile, so aware of how pathetic you are, that sometimes you need to understand what it means to fail. I doubt Cornelius has any idea what this feels like, and it is only through acceptance of this can you become great. Working hard and pushing on will only take you so far.

Patrick:

He has something to prove about something, to someone. I don't know what or why, but I can see it when he runs. There is an intensity over and above that of the natural runner. His shoulders raise, his teeth grit and his gaze focuses forward like he's zoning in on a kill. There's something at the end, some higher goal that he's desperate to reach. Validation, maybe? Proving someone wrong? Proving something to himself? It doesn't look easy, but you can't imagine him ever giving up.

Fabien:

I'll bet he's never even thought about why he does it. He's like a religious fundamentalist who's so wrapped up in their beliefs that they've never considered where they started in the first place. He was first in the egg-and-spoon race at school, first in the club trials, first in the county championships. Everyone loved him, and his mind never turned. He was the teacher's pet. He didn't need to smoke, drink or eat chocolate during breaks. He was doing the 'right' thing, and hey, if he was good at it, then it probably was.

For someone like this, running is simple – perhaps the best sport there is. I think Fabien realised this from about the age of five and I think he still believes it now; however, this is the reason why he's never been as great as he could have been. He simply isn't fucked up enough.

Dwayne:

He operates on a different plain to all the rest of us. He has a rationale in the same way we do, but it is on a rather more spiritual level. One day he explained this to me, midway through a race.

'It's like religious enlightenment Ben, but very real at the same time. It's not an epiphany, cause I haven't found out like…the answers to everything, but it's still a heightened state. When I exercise I can see a new world, full of things that I've never experienced – the stars, the dharma, the universe – and as long as I can keep going, keep running, cycling, swimming or whatever, I can keep it in my sights. That's why I do it Benny-Boy, because one day I am going to find all those things and see what a wonderful place the world is.'

That's the reason for the Mohican. It points to this world and makes him never forget.

I guess I have my own reasons as well. Most of the time I don't think about it, but when the pace starts to increase, they slowly start to come back to me:

Old me – I can't do anything.

Transition – Maybe I can do this.

New me – I can do this. I can do more.

Pain is ———————————— over here. I am here. The pain is behind, in an old me. There is something out there better than pain.

I moved from an unhappy, lethargic self to create a new persona, an active, successful individual. I realised that our identities were as malleable as our muscles and our joints – they get very used to being one way but that doesn't mean you can't turn them into something else. In a box marked 'new' I kept the positives – the happiness, the stamina and the belief – and in a box marked 'old' I put the pain and the negativity. It makes for a simple choice and I always try to choose for the better.

The new 'me' chooses not to concentrate on pain. It isn't pretending pain doesn't exist – it's putting it in a different place and focusing on something else instead, positive things – the race, the minutes-per-mile, the time at the end. Pain and fatigue still exist – over there, but I am here – stronger, better, striving for more.

I run, therefore I am. As long as I keep running, that's okay – I am me, the new me. That's what 'the zone' is all about.

This isn't a case of total mind over matter. There must be some give and take. The human body is capable of incredible things, but it can't do them all the time. I could run pretty fast if there was a madman with a gun at my back, but I can't convince my body to do this whenever it likes. I can only kid it so much.

The towpath passes along the Thames towards Hampton Court Palace. Patrick, Dwayne and Fabien are still ahead of me, but I am biding my time and keeping a good pace. My speed is increasing very, very slowly, meaning I should be able to overtake them soon without breaking any extra sweat. I have them now. Only Fabien is worth worrying about, the rest – no problems.

As the mile approaches Dwayne adjusts his gold necklace, stumbles slightly and inadvertently elbows Patrick in the side. His opponent is forced off the gravel and onto the wet grass, almost slipping as he does so. Dwayne glances quickly over, sees Patrick is okay and then focuses back on the mile marker ahead, leaving Patrick to jump back onto the path and start a long pursuit.

To the old woman walking her dog on the riverbank, this must have seemed like an innocuous incident – two runners trying to find room on a cramped path – however I know different. Yes, it was over in a flash, yes, no-one was hurt and no damage was caused; and yes, Patrick will have suffered nothing more than a second delay; but for a brief moment Patrick will have felt pain, he will have been snapped out of his zone and will now be full of unhelpful emotions. I can hear the anger in his breaths behind me:

Tssssss

Huuur

Tssssss

Huuuur

Tsssssss

Fucker. What did he think he was doing? I am going to hurt him. I may not win this race now, but I don't care. I am going to beat the fucker with the blue Mohican.

Huuur

Tssssss

Huuuur

Tsssssss

It was an elbow in the rib and not a very hard one at that, and I'm sure Dwayne didn't mean to do it, but that doesn't matter. We run with a shield that starts at the top of our thighs and works down to our feet. It dissipates all the screams and cries that come from our legs, even when the hard times kick in, but leaves the rest of us as bare and brittle as balsa. As runners we are bone, muscle and not a lot else, and in the race this becomes even more exposed. The zone is a fragile shell, and if a sharp blow strikes at an unexpected moment, it throws us... and it hurts.

Patrick was in the Ugandan army. He will have a much higher pain threshold than any of us, yet when Dwayne's bony elbow struck him, he reacted like it was a bullet to his heart. It will take him a while to get over this. For the next fifteen minutes he'll be saying to himself:

No pain.

Don't feel pain.

Just run.

No pain.

Pain is failure.

I have a feeling that the pain will make him fail, and I smirk as I hear those breaths behind:

Huuuur

Tssssss

Huuuur

Tssssss

He will feel like he is running fast, but it is only because he is stressed and angry. These emotions waste energy. They will not help him on a half marathon.

I keep up my steady acceleration as Patrick powers past.

Mile up – 5.17. Getting quicker.

MILE 4

The towpath spreads out and a group of four of us forms beside the river. Patrick is leading, but his running style has become increasingly ragged and he cannot stretch away. I am directly behind with Dwayne, and Cornelius has tagged onto the back. Fabien is still a long way ahead, some twenty or thirty metres, and his lead seems to be stretching. My legs sting with the thought of chasing that gap back. We are only four miles through, still happy-time in half marathon terms, so nothing is beyond the realms of possibility, however it's a long way. Slow acceleration is my tactic and I still expect it to work. I believe my body is capable of anything if I give it enough warning.

The course itself has become staggeringly beautiful. To our right, the grounds of Hampton Court Palace, to our left, the Thames and its rhythmic flow; far ahead stands Hampton Court Bridge, where we'll turn and head back into commercial ugliness and hard miles. I try not to think about it and enjoy the peace. Let go. Let the running take me. Let me become the runner.

It's too early. I am still too conscious of my everyday self. Nature is starting to seep in, but it cannot overcome me yet. There's too much of the real-world – stresses, desires, worries, frustrations – stuck in the way.

We are beginning the early exchanges of the trade we will make, mother nature and me. The river, the light gravel underfoot, the manicured gardens of Hampton Court Palace, the sun glinting off the ripples of water. She is just beginning to reward me for my efforts and I'm running faster as a result. I like to believe I'm the only one who feels this, but hey, maybe we all do. Dwayne would understand, Patrick also, but I'm not sure about the others. I'll know later, when I'm stripped of all human comfort, then we'll see just how deep we can all go.

This is not tourist running. I don't appreciate sights and sounds like the people taking pictures in the palace gardens. I'm not here to see or hear, I'm here to race, and all my senses are mixed up in this context. It's like the tree where you had your first kiss or the beach where you proposed to your wife. They're not just trees or beaches, they have greater meaning, they're attached to an emotion inside you. It's the same with the surroundings in the race. The grass and the gravel connect to the physical exertion of my body and we become something together – a cocktail of energy and emotion.

When I pass these places on the train or in the car I get constant déjà-vu from this. I have been to here before but in a different form – the runner – and when the recollection does come, it's always one of warmth and pleasure. That's when I understand the pleasure of running, even if it feels quite the contrary at the time. An incredibly hard race, the feeling...it is second only to the feeling of being in love. Your heart thumps, your emotions swing one way then the other, you yearn and yearn, and then you finally make it. You attain what you desperately desire. That stays with you for a long time.

I speed up and pass Patrick again, and then try and slowly catch Fabien. Cornelius and Dwayne follow me, but I've forgotten about them. I'm looking forward. Hampton Court Bridge. I want to be close to Fabien by then, however far away it is.

My body reacts to the increased cadence – deeper breaths, strain in the calves and hamstrings, less blood in the brain, heart beating faster. Then some food in my stomach starts to move, and a belch of Weetabix forces itself from my mouth. Ugh. I feel a bit sick.

Get down food, stay there. You know you're going to be needed. Digest, like I know you will.

The Runner's Journal Entry 4 – A Runner's Diet

The last meal before a race is a semi-religious experience. The seasoned distance runner will usually eat exactly the same thing at exactly the same time before every race, no matter what. It may seem superstitious, and certainly fastidious, but there are good reasons.

Finding the optimum food required for a race is a difficult process. You want to feel light in order to run fast, but at the same time you need to have a store of energy to call upon during the latter miles when reserves are at their lowest. Essentially you want the impossible, so instead you have to try and find the best fit you can. However, all our bodies are different, so there isn't a simple answer. For what it's worth, here is mine.

The night before the race:

A large plate of pasta with chicken or spinach pesto, eaten in two helpings over the evening.

Some probiotic yoghurt

Lots of water

The morning of the race:

Three Weetabix with semi-skimmed milk, topped with honey.

A cup of green tea

The pasta gives you the carbohydrates which, if the race is longer than 10k, you will need to load up on to get through the last few miles. It might feel like too much, but it isn't. The two or three seconds that you might lose in the first mile from feeling 'heavy,' will be countered by the twenty or thirty seconds you'll gain in the last four or five by having energy left. It works, trust me.

However, you do not want to over-eat, because then you'll feel too sluggish and will not want to race at all. You could also be hit by the dreaded 'stitch' feeling halfway through as well, which you want to avoid at all costs. It is for this reason that I eat this meal in two helpings, rather than just eating less. It should give my body extra time to digest, instead of having everything in one lump.

I tend to stick to white pasta, rather than a wholemeal variety. During a long run your body will need to call on its carbohydrates as quickly as possible, and wholemeal food simply takes too long to break down in a race. Think of the stomach as a bonfire. If you put on a big log then it will burn for longer, but the wood takes a long time to ignite. However, put on smaller sticks and they will burn quickly with larger flames. The fire will fade, but by this time you should have had all the warmth you need. When you are running as fast as you can, you need a constant supply of quick, hot energy, and white pasta is the best thing for this.

Also, you need a sauce. One – because the meal will be pretty unpalatable without one; and two – because you will want to be able to digest it properly and fully. There is no point having all this fantastic carbohydrate if it ends up stuck halfway down your oesophagus. Chewed-up white pasta is also quite a sticky, glutinous substance and you want to be able to help your body to extract the good bits and expend the waste in good time for the morning of the race. I don't want to go too deeply into this, but it is something that plays on all runners' minds before they run, so it needs to be helped in the best way you can. Hence the probiotic yoghurt.

The morning of the race is just as important. Although you'll feel nervous, you'll still need to eat. You need a good breakfast, but not an over-sized one. I recommend some quality food to boost your metabolism, and some sugar for that quick release energy that will make you burst off at the start.

Lastly, the green tea. This is an ideal option, as it will keep you hydrated (as opposed to tea or coffee which will have the opposite effect) and will also promote bowel movement. The latter is not essential – I've run plenty of races when I've been way too tense to go – but it is important to a runner all the same. You want to go before the race if you can, but you don't want to feel totally empty – and you certainly don't want to have to go halfway round. It's a difficult balance. From my experience, pasta has provided the best solution. It sticks well in the stomach to keep you fuelled for the race, but it isn't too hard for the body to digest. Half marathons are tense occasions. Things like this are important, and the more you can do to help any problems, the better.

NB: Long distance running will give rise to some element of gastric movement, and this is something you are just going to have to deal with. I find that as long as you have abstained from spicy foods – and that includes spicy pasta sauce – then you should be just fine.

Finally there is the question of water. During a long race you will need a lot to keep you hydrated, however it is very difficult to take on much at a time. It is therefore essential that you are well-hydrated at the start. The key is to drink a lot of water about forty-five minutes before the race begins, and then not again until about ten minutes to go. This should ensure that any excess is drained away and that you will only need to spend the race topping up, rather than heading straight to the portaloos. Again, it is all about timing.

Nutrition is a very personal thing, so there are no hard-and-fast rules. Before he broke the 3000 metre world record in 1982, Dave Moorcroft ate burger and chips. Usain Bolt eats chicken nuggets. My running coach used to eat two slices of *cake before a race. The routine I've described has seen me through many long races without burning-out or having to stop at the side of the road, but that's only because it works for me. Your body may be very different. Experiment, and see what works for you. Once you figure it out, you'll swear by it for life.*

The moment with the Weetabix passes, but time has been lost. The marker for Mile 5 is approaching and I'm stuck behind Patrick and Cornelius again. Dwayne has dropped back, but Fabien is far away in the distance.

Strangely I'm fine about this. I can get quicker again and pass them, I can feel it. Today is the day. It's a half-a-mile loop around Hampton Court Palace, then up onto the bridge, and then into the town. They'll start to slow, and that's when I'll attack. I have more in my legs, and they won't have an answer.

This hasn't come from nowhere. For the last few months I have lived running – training twice a day, every day, over eighty miles a week – and now it is paying off.

Cornelius has a family; he can't run like I can. Patrick is breathing like a maniac, he will not beat me today. Their running vests aren't targets, they are mere distractions. Only Fabien's red and black means anything to me. Cornelius might think he has the edge, having beaten me in every race we've run together, but he doesn't know who he's up against today. He is dust on my trainers, spittle on my green vest. He might as well not exist.

In distance running it's you and the person in front of you, that's it. There is no time to think of anything else, just the race, the minutes-per-mile and the vest moving up and down ahead.

I see only one. Herne Hill Harriers. Red and black. It is in the water of the Thames, the bus on the bridge, the gates of Hampton Court Palace. Where is he? How long until I pass them all?

Mile 4 up. 5.23. I feel good.

MILE 5

We've been running for...erm...twenty-two minutes I think. One mile at a time. One mile at a time. This is the only way to run a race like this. The mind is not very good at conceiving longevity, so you need to compartmentalize. Just one mile, then we'll deal with the next one. Think about today, not tomorrow. Life, meaning, the wider world, death – these can wait for another time.

The path widens, and I've taken this point to accelerate. There's a water-stop populated by smiling girl guides, but I ignore it. Patrick, Cornelius and the rest might need to drink, but I feel fine. Minutes earlier I was considering how nice the river looked and what time I'd be finished. The fact that I could think like that meant that I wasn't running fast enough. I shouldn't be able to think at all. All I should focus on is taking that next step.

I should have had some water, but I chose not. I'm committed. I'm ready to torture myself and I'm ready for pain and the speed that comes with it. I don't want to look back on the race and think at any point that I wasn't running the hardest I could, because there is no pride in telling yourself that you could have run faster. You need to show it. The tendency to think of yourself as superior is precisely what long-distance running is there to remove, and if you are still proud when you cross the finish line, you haven't tried hard enough. You should be a ruined, pathetic, shadow of a human being.

That's why Cornelius won't win today. He wants to feel good about himself all the time. He will never understand that to feel as good as you can, you must first hit rock bottom and then sink lower. After this, nothing can hurt you, and then you can do whatever you like. I am going to suffer and breathe, suffer and breathe, one mile at a time, until I get to this point. Then I will be superman.

The path passes around the grounds of Hampton Court Palace. Baroque statues look at me from the Privy Garden. I don't want to see them. I don't want to think, but their beauty attracts my gaze. Fountains, flowers and manicured hedges. The grand façade of the palace behind. It's all so opulent, so beautiful, that I lose focus. I feel my body yell:

'STOP. RUNNING. THIS. FAST!'

I focus back on the path ahead. I'm not listening.

Then my mind tries to rationalize things.

This is not a good idea. You are running almost five-minute mile pace. You know you can't run this fast. You know what will happen if you do. Think about your pace and your cadence.

I try not to hear. I keep running and concentrate on breathing. I am a machine, and I don't know how to run slower.

You can't run this fast. This is not how to run a half marathon. You can't even run a 10k this quickly. Stop it. Stop it now.

I can. I can run this fast and I will keep doing so. It is only fear that gives me boundaries. I'm scared of the pain, but the pain might not even come. How do I know until I am there?

To be a runner, is to remember that there are no boundaries to what you can do. You just need to try harder.

I can run this fast. Only if I think, will I convince myself otherwise.

Don't think.

Don't think.

Don't think.

Breathe.

Breathe.

Breathe.

Muscles move, heart beats, lungs inhale.

This is it.

This is all running is.

THE ROAD RUNNER

We have been runners since we were apes.

Breathe in.

Breathe out.

Breathe in.

Breathe out.

Thoughts come again.

Block them. Cover them with blackness.

Crowds gather by the side of the river. A group of children are holding a banner with 'Come on Dad!' written in bold pink letters. 'Come on, keep going!' they shout

Shut up. Shut the fuck up. Stop fucking clapping. Don't distract me. Don't let me think.

'Well done. You're second. You're doing really well!'

Hampton Court Palace. Pompous, baroque nightmare. Keep going, don't think about it.

'Come on. You can do it. Not far to go!'

Breathe.

Grit teeth.

Breathe again.

What time? How quick am I going? Where's the next mile marker?

The Runner's Journal Entry 5 – The 5k problem

It's the most popular distance for running in the country by quite a long way. Not too daunting for beginners, still a worthwhile challenge for professionals, the 3.15-mile course provides a perfect route into all forms of endurance athletics. Each weekend there are hundreds of 5k races taking place, and the level of participation is increasing all the time. And yet for a specialist half marathon runner – and I think for most 'proper' distance runners – it is not quite the true running experience. For some, it is not a distance run at all.

I started running with a 5k. I was roped into it after a bet at the pub which I instantly regretted. However, after putting in a reasonably quick time around my local park, I found that running was something I had a natural aptitude for. I wanted to continue and I wanted to do better. That's the clever thing about the 5k, it's not far enough to put you off, but at the same time it never really satisfies.

Now I love the challenge of pushing my body to the limit and then trying to push it even further. I love letting my problems flow through my feet and into the pavement below. I love the meditative state you reach when your body runs out of energy. I love the joy of seeing the finishing line, and the punishment of forcing yourself to reach it a minute faster. I love seeing the world move beside me and feeling my body float over it while my legs run beneath. I love all of this. And I hate the 5k because it removes all of this from the running experience.

The 5k is the cheese-lover's Edam, the car enthusiast's Ford Fiesta, the lyric poet's bawdy verse. It is a pale imitation of the real thing, a manufactured product missing all the goodness of the pure form. It is marathon running for the masses, and as such it removes all the special pleasures that the sport can invoke.

There are reasons for this. First, a 5k is not very long. Now I'm not coming over all elitist-runner here – I don't think everyone should be able to complete a sixty-mile ultra-marathon with one leg tied behind their backs – but in order to appreciate the true experience of running you need to be covering a distance of at least ten kilometres. Before that, your body will not reach the level of fatigue to attain the Zen-like euphoria that running can bring. You also will be unable to gain that panoramic vision of distance and time, which stretches your conception of who you are and what you can do. And at the end you should feel that sense of achievement, that you have done something beyond the capacity of the average human. Running 5k is not an exceptional achievement, like it or lump it.

Second, in order to run a 5k in a fast time, you need to approach it as if you were not even running a distance race at all. It is a race that is included in the Olympic track events and is therefore much more about speed and leg power than endurance, and should be treated as such. The essence of the race lies more in the sprint disciplines such as the 100 or 200 meters, rather than the full or half marathon. This is something that has taken me a long time to accept, and it has led me to treat the race in a very different way. Rather than preparing for a tactical and mental rollercoaster (as I would in a half marathon for example), the 5k is a matter of simple procedure:

Warm up

Stand at the start

Run as fast as you can

Keep going and hope for the best

Your pace needs to be at an entirely different level to a long-distance race because essentially you shouldn't be pacing yourself at all. In a 5k you should not be able to think about how fast you are running, because if you are, you are not running fast enough. It is a race run at anaerobic threshold all the way, not just for the first or last kilometer, but for the whole thing. The fact is that a 5k can be run at one pace all the way because it is ONLY three-and-a-bit miles, and your body is perfectly capable of maintaining that if you really want it to.

You know that speed in a half marathon that hurts? The one that you know is too fast and that you should only consider running for a minute or two at a time? That's 5k pace, all the way. Do you like running that pace? Do all your worries drift away? Do you become one with the world around you?

I didn't think so.

It feels more like sprinting because in terms of distance running this is exactly what the 5k is. And at the end of the day that isn't distance running at all, it is track running, which is either to your taste or isn't. The purest may disagree — where are the tactics? the bend speed? the final sprint? — but as an endurance runner I know my sport and I know a 5k is different.

It seems to me that the 5k is an athletics genre all on its own — a link between the two disciplines of track and distance — but one which the practitioners of both of these arts, disdain as a mediocre form of the other.

The simple facts are that a 5k is accessible, manageable and enjoyable, and therefore perfect for an entry into all manners of athletics. For the experienced athlete it is also excellent training whatever their persuasion — speed work for the marathon runners, an endurance test for the middle-distance athletes, a good tempo run for a longer race.

I don't hate the 5k. It is a convenient distance for training and a fun event to compete in socially. However, it is not distance running as I know it.

Maybe I just need to accept it for what it is, and then I'll start to enjoy it more. I don't know if I want to spend months training for it, but I like the way it gives me a taste of all the feelings that a longer race can evoke, without giving the full experience. It is hard and intense, and it leaves one wholly unsatisfied at the end.

Maybe that's the perfect running experience of all.

There are still no thoughts. I feel dizzy. Electrons fire around my nervous system, trying to find a place for their desperate messages, but I block them out. This is fight or flight. I am switching them off so that I can concentrate on just one thing – survival.

For the runner this is the optimum place to be, but it is a miserable, awful place, and not one that any human can stay in for long, no matter how much they force themselves. To get there in the first place is an achievement – you will have to convince your body that the race is more important than death, and that it must keep going no matter what. It is like drowning in the sea, gasping your last breath, but then refusing the offer of a lifebelt. This is not an easy way to reason, but that is how the runner thinks, or certainly the runner moving at a fast pace. Will I push myself to the point of death? That depends just how good an endurance runner I want to be.

The road turns onto Hampton Court Bridge and the mile is almost up.

Breathe.

Breathe.

Breathe.

It is easier now I can see the line.

5.07. Keep breathing

MILE 6

I'm back. There is only so long you can live beyond your limits. The body will always fight back, no matter what you do. Fabien is thirty metres up the road and I'm catching at a rate that I would never have expected. The last mile was fast – too fast – but still I need to try and keep as close to that pace as possible. If I know I can do it, then I can do it again.

This is how you get quicker and how you progress as a runner – by finding out what you can do, reaching your limit and then doing it again and again and again, until you can push yourself even more. It's hard, but if you can continue to do it, then the entire running world can be at your disposal. The National Championships? The Worlds? The Olympics? Keep pushing. Do you reach a plateau? Is there a point where as a runner you simply cannot go any faster? Can you run the perfect race? The possibilities are endless.

I guess that's what we are all striving for as runners, the absolute limit, but I'm not sure whether it truly exists. Like everything else we do as humans, running is a fundamentally futile exercise. It has desperate lows, incredible highs, but at the end of it there is a general feeling of dissatisfaction. We can always do better. Our personal bests are times waiting to be beaten. We'll never be perfectly happy, but the journey will be an experience like no other. Perhaps this is the most perfect pleasure of all.

I'm currently in the position where I'm running quicker than I have before, and it's an exciting place to be. The world has opened out in front of me and I can go wherever I want. I am never going to be comfortable running 5.30 mile pace anymore because I will always know that I can do better. It's a frightening thought. Nothing is ever going to be easy again.

Why? Why have I done this? Why can't I ever just be happy?

At the front, the race is always hard. Always.

I follow Fabien as the course passes away from the river and into suburbia. Crowds of people have gathered outside their homes to cheer us on. They see that I am catching him, and their volume increases. The encouragement flows through my body and I run quicker again.

Breathe.

Breathe.

Breathe.

It's comfortable now. The doubts are disappearing. The crowd are giving me energy. Fabien won't listen to them – he doesn't care – but I feel motivated. I can use their voices.

'Come on!'

'Keep going!'

'You're almost with him!'

I can go faster.

The Runner's Journal Entry 6 – A Marathon Watch

'So why are you standing out here today?' a man in an anorak asks me. 'Do you know someone running?'

'No' I say.

'Are you supporting one of the leaders?'

'No.'

'Are you working for one of the charities?'

'No.;

'Oh,' my inquisitor shrugs. 'So why are you down here today then?'

'I just like it,' I tell him. 'I like watching.'

I've been coming to watch the marathon for a decade now. At first it was a whim, but now I won't miss it for the world.

I'm not really a running fan or anything. I don't know who any of the leaders are, unless it's Mo Farah of course, and I don't know how fast they go or even what a good time is. That's not why I'm here.

The two times I have actually known people running, I didn't see them go past, or even look for them if I'm honest about it. That's not why I'm here either.

I watch the marathon because I like the way it makes me feel. The world can be a pretty miserable place 364 days a year, and London in particular. Everyone is getting on with their day-to-day lives, always busy, always trying to squeeze everything in, never having time for themselves or for other people. Then marathon day comes and everything changes.

It begins with the runners — 38,000 people all gearing up to do something harder than anything they have before. They're all different — rich and poor, black and white — but on the start line of the race they are all the same — nervous, scared and desperate to get running. On such a free psychological playing field there is no preconception or dominance because no-one can be entirely confident with a twenty-six mile road ahead of them. Everyone is equal.

I sense this when I walk down to the Victoria Embankment this Sunday morning — all of London forgetting if they are man or woman, black or white, lawyer or dustman, and embarking on a great adventure together. The same sites are here — Big Ben, Canary Wharf, Tower of London — but they are nothing but buildings along the route, shapes ignored by the blinkers of exertion.

I stop by Somerset House, about two miles from the finish. Beside me stand charity workers, policemen, schoolchildren and families, all out to support and urge the runners on. I like to watch them as much as the runners themselves, raised like meerkats, looking for their loved ones or minor celebrities, but cheering everyone on as they pass, whether they need it or not.

The elite runners come through first. Even though they are the highly trained and superfit, they cannot hide the grit and determination they need to get through the final miles. There is no pride here, no arrogance. None of these runners are here for the show. You can see it in the bodies – all skin, bone and muscle, like a medical wall chart – the bare essence of a human being. I think that's why they look so natural when they run – graceful, like a horse or a cheetah – they are doing something that humans are built to do, doing it in a perfect way, and their bodies reflect this. We cheer them on, but they seem unable to hear us. Their faces are aimed forward, relentlessly focused on the finish line.

After a while, I head into Trafalgar Square to eat a spot of lunch, less I be overcome by the energy of the running gods. Groups of people walk past towards St James Park – students with cases of beer, families waiting for mum or dad, shoppers caught up in the aura of goodness – all of them talking and laughing, holding banners or buckets of sweets. It is crowded like the Tube at rush hour, but there is not a face of irritation amongst them. On marathon day, small gripes seem irrelevant.

I have a cheese sandwich, then follow them into the park. The route runs along Birdcage Walk on the south side, before turning up to Buckingham Palace and the long final stretch along The Mall. There are thousands of people here, supporting the athletes whether they know them or not.

'Come on Elvis!' we cheer.

'Come on Dave,' we yell.

'Keep going Fred Flintstone!'

Yes, it's funny. Yes, the sight of a grizzled man in a tutu with tears in his eyes is a wonderful thing, but we are cheering to encourage as well. The honesty in the runners' faces is too much for anything else. Even in a gorilla outfit you can see the emotions come through:

It hurts.

Oh God it hurts.

I can't carry on.

All these runners – athletes and non-athletes, make us helplessly aware of our fallibility as humans, and humble us into good-humour and altruism. We feel that we must take part, even if it involves sitting on the grass, getting drunk and raising the occasional hand-clap – at least we are doing something to help them along.

People are nice. We don't like to be told to do it, or forced to do it, but if we can throw the lifebelt of our own accord, then we will.

This is why we support them, and why we enjoy doing it – because they need it, because it makes a difference to them and because as humans, we are good. That's why the human race prevails, because inside us all is a need to help each other through adversity, to get us over the finish line.

For years living in London I hadn't believed this was true. I thought everyone was just out for themselves. But this was before I saw the marathon – the runners stretched to the limit, the crowds full of magnanimity, the shared happiness at the finish.

As I sit in the park, watching the runners meet up with their families, brandish medals, sip on Lucozade, hug one and all, I realise this is why we all feel so good. The marathon reminds us who we are as humans. There is no pretense, nothing contrived – we are just us, and at the end of it all, we are all the same.

Tomorrow, when the barriers are folded up, the tents are taken down and the police are back walking the beat, all of this will be forgotten. We will ignore each other, stand in queues, clench our fists when the man in front takes the last place on the tube, but somewhere deep inside we'll feel okay because we'll know that the marathon will be back soon, and people will be happy once again.

The crowd thickens as we continue north towards Kingston town centre. It's coming up to ten in the morning and the normal people have come out to support the freaks punishing themselves. I can feel their eyes looking with amused awe. What are they doing to themselves? How can they do this for fun? Why do they want to feel pain? I want to tell them how great it is. If they were to run, they would feel like this. They are missing out on so much.

They cheer us as we pass, then go back to their coffees and croissants. That's their life. That's how they run. It's okay, but it's not the same.

Without thinking I have almost caught Fabien up. His black and red and vest is only ten metres in front. I could lasso him and drag him back if I wanted to. It won't be long before I'm alongside.

It is hard when you are winning, and even harder when the crowds are around cheering for the person behind you. If you are in front you must always run your own race, but when the crowd urging for you to be caught, this becomes almost impossible. Their shouts and claps build in your head like a roll of thunder. They don't see this as your own individual run – the way you should see it – they see it as a race, and as the clapping and cheering increases, you start to believe them.

'Keep going!' they say to me. 'He's right in front you.'

'Come on green vest!' they shout. 'Come on, you can catch him!'

Fabien is dragged back with every shout. His stride falters, his breathing changes and he checks his stride. Negative thoughts cloud his mind.

The world wants me to lose.

The crowd is against me.

Something is wrong.

He shakes his head, trying to ignore them and stay in his zone, but it's impossible. It's like being sat in a crowded room, when suddenly everyone turns to look at something out the window.

'Look,' they say. 'Look at that. You have to look.'

But you don't want to look. You want to keep your mind focused on what you're doing.

'Look,' they repeat. 'God, look, you must look.'

You try again to focus, to stare at your desk, at the table. Anything but to look out the window.

Then they nudge you and push you and turn your head with their hands.

'Look. Look out. Look out now!'

You start to let yourself go. You're so concerned with them persuading you to look out, that you forget why you don't want to look in the first place.

'Go on. Go on, look!'

Until you finally give in and look.

In the run it's the same. You try and proceed as you are – the same pace, the same breathing, the same mindset – but when a hundred voices are cheering, you can't help but listen. That's when you look behind you and snap out of the zone – and that's when you are caught.

The crowd are affecting me as well. I am running faster than I should be, but I convince myself it doesn't matter. They are giving me strength. They are transferring their energy to me. I am stronger. I can catch Fabien, Surrey's number one.

I sprint through the mile barrier, and almost forget to check my watch.

5.10. I will pay for this.

MILE 7

Fabien has let me catch up. The smooth, ultra-confident Surrey champion has surrendered to Ben Evans, the naïve journeyman, who no-one in athletics has ever paid any attention to. He might have noticed that I'm in better shape than ever before, but I'm sure Fabien didn't think I'd mount a serious challenge. Maybe he still believes this, and he's waiting for me to crack. Ben doesn't run this fast. I'll let him have his fun. He'll burn out sooner or later. He doesn't know how to win.

I want to prove Fabien wrong, but the moment we leave the crowds I start to doubt myself. Catching him is only the start. To put together a lead I'll need to maintain my current pace or speed up, which I'm not sure I have it in me to do. Maybe I should try and break Fabien now and pull away? Would I just break myself? Should I bide my time while the road is long and dull, or should I just go? I am quick enough. I am quick enough. My body can take it.

I speed away for a few seconds and then slow back to a comfortable 5.25 pace again.

It's too early. I won't go yet. It's time to relax.

The Runner's Journal Entry 7 – A Village Run

It's May bank holiday. It's ten in the morning. It's raining torrentially. As this is England, the majority of the population is still in bed watching TV in their pants. They are certainly not standing in a village green wearing shorts and a vest, stretching their calves against the side of a tree and warming up for a morning race. No, there must be something very, very strange about these people.

We're here for the Elstead Marathon, a 5.4 mile race, in the heart of leafy Surrey. It's organized by the local scout group and has been running over the same route – woods, common, river crossing – for over a hundred years. No-one knows why they call it a marathon, and no-one knows why it ends with a knee-deep wade through the River Wey, but this is how the race always is, and it attracts runners from all over the country, aspiring to have their names engraved on the winners' plaque in The Golden Fleece pub.

I'm not sure what I'm doing here. As I look around at the competitors huddled together on what we assume to be the start line, I feel very out of place. These people aren't runners. This isn't a proper running race.

In the traditional, serious races the participants are a familiar breed – lean, muscly individuals wearing club outfits and looking very serious and focused. They are proper, elite athletes who run a hundred miles a week, and they train specifically to achieve a certain time over a certain distance. They are not there for fun. But in the race today these athletes are conspicuous by their absence. It is a much more…human affair.

The field comprises the fat and the thin, old and young and the fit and the not-so-fit. There is a team from the local gym and a team from the local kebab house. There is a six-year-old kid running with his dog and an eighty-year-old man running with his stick. Most of them would rather be in bed watching TV, or hungover, or even in church. None of them want to be out in the rain. None of them want to run a 5.4 mile race.

Today the man to beat is Vincent Kemp. He has won this event for the last five years and is strong favourite to win again. No-one has ever come close, and I think even if they could, they wouldn't want to beat him. It just wouldn't be the right thing to do. As the town crier walks over to announce the start of the race crowds of people chant his name.

'Go Vincent! Go Vincent!'

None of these people, not even Vincent, are like the people I race with in the city. They look different, they sound different and they wear different expressions on their faces. Vincent doesn't seem particularly fit, and even as we prepare for the start, he is smiling and joking along with the other competitors. There is none of the usual intensity – no nervous shuffling of feet or readjusting of stopwatches – and when the town crier says 'Go!' we go, simple as that. No-one is prepared and no-one seems to care how fast they are going. I seem to be the only one wearing a watch.

The pace starts fast, and with a minute or so, the course turns up a steep hill and onto a horrible muddy track. I'm breathing hard and struggling to keep up a good rhythm. It shouldn't be this hard, but for some reason no-one seems to have slowed down. How can they all be this fast?

Quite soon I notice that everyone else seems to be finding it much easier. A man passes me whilst adjusting his wedding dress, a teenager breezes ahead whilst listening to music on his headphones and a bearded man scuttles up whilst his dog chases enthusiastically behind. No-one seems to care about the time or the gradient, but yet...yet they are all running very, very fast. I am a seasoned city racer, wearing trail flats and a Lycra top. I should be streaming ahead at the front, but the complete opposite is happening..

How can they be so quick? I think to myself.

Look at their awful techniques!

What a stupid course.

I'll bet they make it like this, so outsiders can't win.

The more I pass blame, the more I tense up and the harder the hills become. In their relaxed and idiosyncratic way, the home athletes overtake over and over. I drop back into fifth, tenth, thirteenth place. The mud saps the energy from legs.

Finally we emerge from the trees, and I feel the worst is over. A long road section ahead, surely this must be when I can catch up?

Then the contest becomes even more ludicrous.

Ten of the runners who have overtaken me have stopped at a table on the side of the course and are downing pints of beer, served by the local brewery. Yes, beer – that cardinal sin of the super-healthy modern athlete – being downed by runners who so far appear to have considerably more stamina than me.

Here it is, I think to myself. Here's my chance. There's no way they'll be able to stay ahead of me now.

I sprint past and move into second place, with the curly black hair of Vincent Kemp in my sights. There are three miles to go. It won't be long before the serious, civilized runner will show the village idiot how to win.

The course turns into the woods and back into the mud. Through gasps and gags,

I try to stay on Vincent's tail. Surely he won't be able to keep this up? Surely he has to slow down soon?

Then I become aware of a noise behind me, the sound of bounding, bouncing feet.

They're catching me up. Despite downing pints of beer, they can still run quicker than me. How is this possible?

Then another noise reverberates around the trees, a noise which I know well but have never heard uttered halfway through a race. It is the sound of casual conversation.

'So I hear The Cockerel's going to close.'

'Shame, I used to love it in there on a Sunday. Liz behind the bar in particular.'

The voices are familiar – I heard them only minutes ago, but surely they cannot be real? Not in the middle of a race? A few moments later a wedding dress, a large pair of headphones, a wrinkled neck and a chubby backside, all pass me in one leisurely gallop.

'...and then she nudged me in the side,' one says. 'And told me I'd find my trousers in the back yard!'

'Ha, ha!'

'I guess there is plenty of room to spare down there.'

Then they are gone, leaving my flailing, helpless body behind.

As we turn down the hill with a hundred metres to go, the cheers below tell me that Vincent has already won. I take a slow, sad wade through the freezing river and trudge towards the village green, the cushioning in my shoes squeaking with every step. It's only now that I can accept what I have known all along. This race is different. The runners aren't like those back home. The course is nothing like city circuits, parks and streets. But most of all running itself is different.

To me, running is a means to challenge yourself. It is a way to focus your mind, to escape from the pressures of the world, to be healthier and fitter, and a winner.

But here it is nothing of the sort. Here running is something completely different – it's fun. There's no complications – goals, targets or times – it's just a run around a village. Vincent Kemp wins and everyone else enjoys themselves. That's the way it's always been and that's how it will be for another twenty years.

As I approach the finish line my shoulders relax, my arms lighten, and I start to laugh. None of it matters – the time, the course, the position – I just need to enjoy it. They're right - running should be fun.

I sprint the last mile quicker than I have ever run a mile before. There isn't any pressure to win, or to get a time and to beat a certain person, and somehow this enables me to fly over the village green. I am relaxed – and happy.

Maybe this is how we should always run – with a smile on our faces, not caring about the time or the result at the end. Maybe racing shouldn't always be about striving to be number one, it should be about enjoying the event and having fun on a Sunday morning. When we realise this, it's amazing how much happier we can become.

See you next year, Vincent. Mine's a pint of bitter.

Fabien looks over at me. He isn't interested in relaxing. I can feel the heat of his breath and his legs moving in time with mine. He is sucking my energy – a parasite, a fucking parasite – and with each stride a chill runs down the back of my neck. Everything was good, but now all my power and my confidence is being sucked away by a leech dressed in black and red. I am drowning in a lake and there is nothing to grab onto – a long road of office buildings and car showrooms. All the while he keeps going:

Suck. Suck. Suck.

Suck. Suck. Suck.

The running becomes harder and my speed becomes slower and slower. I am pushing again but it is different now. This isn't the burst of acceleration that I had over Hampton Court Bridge, but a long slog in which I'm merely maintaining pace – a pace that's getting harder with every step.

I need something to drag me closer to the end. This middleness is so terminal. I've used so much energy and there is still so far to go. It feels like purgatory, with no past to contemplate and no future to aspire to, and with Fabien as my tormenter. God, I hate him, in his red and black vest; I hate him more than anyone, more than that hippie Dwayne or that smug prick Cornelius. I hate him because he's trying to hold me back and suck my blood. He can't have me. I'm not for sharing.

I increase my pace to below the five-minute mile mark to try and escape. The road stretches out further in front of me. Cars float on the horizon like ships in the ocean. Chevrons stretch into infinity. Time slows, and every second is painful. It's a bad moment and a bad mile. I need to accept this and I will get through.

Amidst the suffering I try to think of something worse. I'm stuck in a room and I can't get out. It's a long meeting that will go on all day. All my bosses are in there, looking at me. I'm sweating and shaking, and I can't make it stop.

Then I remember something my psychologist said:

'You need to breathe and breathe, and you need to think – I am going to get through this. There is an end to this. I need to be calm and everything will be okay. No feeling lasts forever.'

I think about this as I run through the end of this concrete mile. It's bad, it's empty and it's desolate, but it will not last forever. I will get through this and it will get better. My mind will clear. Life is not one thing or the other; it is a series of unpredictable feelings and events which will be bad and good, but never permanent. I will leave this road. I will not be on mile seven forever and Fabien will not stay directly behind me forever. As long as I keep going something will change. That's how life works.

There are moments worse than this. I need to appreciate how much worse it could be. I'm breathing, I'm alive and I'm running a race. I don't need to speed up or slow down – I need to keep where I am and keep going. It's that simple. Keep going. Nothing else.

Don't think again. Stop the thoughts and you'll be fine. No Fabien, no first second or third. Just the next mile. Just the next mile.

It takes a long time. The suburban monotony of red-brick houses, pubs and churches appear over and over. The road winds along like we are stuck in a film reel. The world is a middle-class morass. My soul is dead. But I run. I run through and Fabien follows, and we reach the mile marker. Mile eight. A turn back to the Thames. Hell is over. I can breathe again.

5.25. Not as fast as I thought. It's over. I don't care.

MILE 8

The hardest part is over. Four miles to go, not including this one. I can feel the end is coming. I can run this distance in my sleep.

We are directed down a bike path and then back onto the side of the Thames. The path becomes concrete and follows the flow of the river back into London. A light wind blows behind us. Sparrows chirp in the trees. Nature is on our side. It's running paradise.

The sun reflects off an eddy on the water's surface. It's the river winking, telling me that I have its support. I am the river and the river is me. We run together, flow together. Movement is good. Movement is the journey.

Fabien feels it too. As soon as we come onto the towpath, he increases his pace and overtakes me. His vest is red with the blood of my body, and black with the remnants of my soul. I want them back. I will not let him escape with my body and my feelings. You're mine Fabien, I'm not letting you get away.

A hit of lactic acid shoots through my thighs.

Hate.

I hate you.

I run because I hate.

Because it feels good.

The course passes under Kingston Bridge. On the opposite bank I can see the slower runners trotting towards Hampton Court. They smile and chat and listen to music. One is dressed as a fireman. They seem to know each other and have collective spirit. They don't seem to care who wins or loses. If anything, they seem to be enjoying themselves.

Why can't I be like them? Why does it matter if I win or lose?

The Runner's Journal Entry 8 – Parkrun

To 'parkrun.' To be a 'parkrunner.' This is a new term in the running vernacular in the last five years – one that does not fit in with the conventional image of teenagers sprinting round a track, or overweight men huffing and puffing around the park.

Parkrunning is now an integral part of the sport of running, much more so than the traditional arenas of track meetings or local cross-country races. Hundreds of thousands compete every week, wind rain or shine, in hundreds of different locations throughout the UK. It is one of the fastest growing sporting pursuits in the country. Why is this? Why do so many people want to 'parkrun? Who are they, this new breed of sportsperson?

Running in the twenty-first century is generally an individual pursuit. Some still take part to beat the competition, but for most it is a way to get fit, to relieve stress, to forget about the working day, to get out into nature and to feel a bit more human after a day spent in front of the computer.

Parkrunning takes this, then adds a sense of community. Runners are encouraged to enjoy themselves, to chat as they run, to meet up at the finish, to go for coffee and cake at a local café. They should not exist in their running bubbles, like the serious athletes do.

So why does it work? Who do so many people who run alone ninety percent of the time, decide to run in a such a social atmosphere on a Saturday morning? How does parkrun create such a community, in our self-orientated world?

The reason, I think, lies in why we run in the first place.

Running, as an adult, is a little embarrassing. Many of us do it to escape something or change something we don't like about ourselves. Doing it is, in a way, an admission of inadequacy in some form or another.

I'm overweight. I'm going to get thinner.

I'm unfit, I'm going to get fitter.

I'm unhappy. I'm going to get happy.

However, at the same time it is a very positive activity. We are accepting our faults and are trying to change them. We're making an effort to improve ourselves.

Then we decide to check out a parkrun, and we realise that there are hundreds of other people doing this too. It isn't a bunch of svelte young athletes in tight shorts who never had a problem in their lives, it's a community of adults making an effort to feel good, about themselves and about life.

You want to lose weight? Hey, me too!

You run because it makes you happy? Hey, me too!

You run to meet new people? Hey, me too!

The key word here is 'effort.' A parkrun is not a race. Almost no-one turns up on a Saturday morning with a view of trying to win. However, it is not the same as a night down the pub – there is effort involved. Parkrunners are not simply chewing the fat over a few beers – they are physically expressing their desire to feel better, striving to achieve whatever personal goal they have laid down for themselves.

Here is where the safe, open environment of a parkrun is important, that whatever our personal goal, be it a nineteen minute 5k or a thirty-nine minute *one, then it's okay, it's to be respected and celebrated either way.*

Parkrun is, in this way, a microcosm of how we would like modern life to be — a shared experience, a collective effort to keep going, to improve, one that will become easier if we share it with each other.

So here lies the reason why parkrunning has tapped into the national consciousness in a way traditional competitive running has not. It respects the reasons people engage with the sport. It isn't about winning, it is about achieving personal goals. It celebrates each participant as an individual, rather than who is the first across the line.

If we were to define what it is, I think we could say the following:

parkrun (verb) — to be human in the twenty-first century. To share this with others. To be alive together.

Fabien and I continue to push each other, neither willing to show weakness. Acid builds in my stomach and I'm forced to take deeper and deeper breaths to compensate.

Fabien looks behind. He's hoping I'm not there. He's suffering too.

I increase my pace to move alongside. There's no emotion registered on his face, but his fists are clenched and his shoulders are tense. He is struggling more than he thought. I could help and move in front of him for a while, but I don't want to. Fabien wouldn't help me out.

The path continues along the river. Rowing boats race along the water, heading back towards Kingston Bridge. The sun glints off the oars. I narrow my eyes and focus on the path ahead. Sweat drips from my forehead.

The path climbs gently onto the upper towpath. There's a line of trees up ahead.

Come on Fabien. Come on, lead us into the darkness.

The river disappears, the sky fades and the gravel turns to a rough path. I feel better again. It is just the two of us. We are in a different world where nothing else exists.

Fabien checks back and ups the pace again. He is using me, telling himself that whatever is happening in his mind, he must stay in front. He is used to being a leader. He understands what it means to constantly affirm power and control – and he enjoys it. He is arrogant enough to believe it's his burden to take on. He won't let me dent his pride.

Through the trees we continue, nudging through branches, leaping over puddles, cutting each other up and bellowing at casual walkers who dare to cross our path. In the woods it isn't a race, it is a battle. The rules of the road have gone.

I overtake at the next patch of mud. Fabien passes back as we descend under a bridge. We run apart to avoid a large dog, then sprint together as the path opens.

Suburbia is approaching. The mile marker is ahead, on the corner of a terraced street. A group of supporters are gathered at the end of the path. They cheer loudly as we approach.

Fabien looks over at me and shakes his head.

What? I think to myself. What's your problem? Don't you want to race anymore?

He clenches his fists, checks behind and then ups the pace.

The crowd cheer, even louder than before.

Fabien looks back again.

What's happening? Why are you so concerned all of a sudden?

'Come on!' shout the crowd. 'Come on, they're only just ahead of you.'

Then I realise what's happened. They're not cheering for us. We're the leaders. They're cheering for someone else.

I don't want to look.

Fabien checks behind once more, then sprints on ahead.

I don't want to look.

The crowd cheer once more.

I don't want to look. I don't want to know.

I can't help it.

We approach the mile marker.

I quickly check behind.

Fuck.

Cornelius and Patrick are storming up the path towards us, with Dwayne following behind.

I turn away and look over to the river. It is black and still.

The end is coming. They are demons, emerging the Styx to invade our world – mine and Fabien's. Our two-mile affair is over.

5.25 – not fast enough.

MILE 9

It can't be happening, it simply cannot be happening. I have run harder than ever today and yet still they are going to catch me. What is the point? Why do I bother? Why is it never fast enough?

Patrick and Cornelius glide towards us over the concrete. I want to have the urge to fight and try to hang on, but as they come closer and closer, I'm so low that I let them through without a look. I hate myself. I hate the race.

There are still four miles to go and I'm broken. I simply cannot run faster than this, and if it isn't good enough, then I might as well let them go. I might as well give up, because I will never be better.

Fabien seems to feel the same way. As Cornelius saunters alongside and Patrick gives a smug look over, Fabien does not even flinch. He runs just as he always has, smooth and measured, with his eyes focused on the path ahead and his shoulder relaxed. It is the way we all should run – concentrating on our own race – but the way none of us do, not in a half marathon anyway. Maybe he's at his limit as well. Maybe he knows that looking will not make any difference. Maybe he has nothing left either.

Cornelius and Patrick disappear up the road. I don't think I'll ever to be able to catch them.

For one minute, ONE minute I thought that victory was within my grasp. When we turned off that last hellish mile and headed into the trees, I felt like I had the edge, that this time I was going to be ahead of the rest of them, but...well, I'd been naive as usual. What did I think they'd been doing over the last six months – sitting at home watching TV? Eating kebabs? Of course not. We are all runners, we are all trying to be the best we can at it, and we will probably never stop trying until our legs give way or our hearts give up. Patrick may look ungainly and untrained, all wide eyes and flailing limbs, but he is still a runner. Cornelius? Hadn't he semi-retired to become a working dad? Of course not. He is still running, and he is still trying to be the best runner there is. Fabien? Running is his life. That's why he can concentrate like he does – because there is nothing else to distract him. And Dwayne? I'm not sure what he is, but he can do anything he wants – and he wants to run.

Am I different to these people? I don't think so. In fact, the only difference is that they are better than me. They have all won races, they all know what it takes. I am still Ben Evans from Guildford – four second-places and counting. Nice guy but not a winner. Too normal to have a cutting edge. Too nice. Kids himself that he is better than he is. Runs for Guildford and Godalming. Who are they?

The Runner's Journal Entry 9 – A Club Meeting

It was the first race meet of the season and things were not going well. Darren, our sole hope for the 100m, 200m, 400m long jump, triple jump, hurdles and pole vault, was injured.

'I don't know how it happened,' he said, hobbling up the finishing straight. 'I jogged here from the station to warm up and something just went. I don't know how, but…I don't think I can run on it.'

In the three years I had been with the club, this had never happened. According to legend, Darren hadn't missed a meet since his twenty-fifth birthday, two decades previously, and running without him was almost unthinkable. With a full team available I would do the 5000m and the 1500m, Tim the 800m, Aaron the high jump, Mike the discus and shot put, James the steeplechase, and Darren did everything else. Most of the time someone wouldn't show up – I ran marathons much of the time and Mike was frequently in jail – but Darren would be there no matter what.

James, our most 'senior' athlete, immediately made efforts to solve the problem. As an ex-international 400m runner in his day (for Wales), he tended to assume the position of captain, if such a thing was ever required, and he brought us together for a team huddle. 'Right chaps,' he said. 'You can see what's happened here, and it's not good news. Darren's a key part of our team, but don't worry, we can go on without him. We had a similar situation to this back in the Commonwealths in 74.' He pulled out a pair of running shoes from a carrier bag and placed small strips of paper inside one of them. 'And this is how we solved it.'

The shoe was placed in the middle of the circle.

'What…draw lots?' asked Mike, the twenty-stone former bodyguard.

'Yep,' said James. 'It didn't do us any harm. I reached the final of the pole vault in Edmonton without ever having tried it before.'

'Bollocks,' said Mike, reaching into the shoe. 'That wasn't even an event back then…oh fuck. Hurdles? You got to be having a laugh.'

'We need the points,' James said. 'I don't care if you take twenty seconds or twenty minutes, if you cross that line we get a point. And need I remind you that last year we escaped relegation by just…'

'ONE POINT,' we chorused.

Our club had been in division two of the Surrey league since 1963 and last year was the closest we'd ever come to being relegated. In terms of the club's history, we were officially the worst ever performers, and were very proud of our achievement.

'What is Surrey athletics all about?' continued James.

'COMPETING,' we said.

'Exactly. Competing, not winning'

This was the only way athletics at this level could survive. In fact, sometimes I was amazed it did at all. The Surrey league was one of the top competitions in the country, where the likes of Martin Rooney, Jason Livingstone and Gary Staines had plied their trade, but yet the track-meets, of which there were only five a season, felt more like boozy pub cricket matches rather than showcases for potential Olympic talents. Teams would gather under sun awnings alongside families munching sandwiches; children ran across the track and played in the long jump pit; then once every few minutes, a race took place. These were normally rather predictable affairs, with two or three athletes streets ahead of the rest, a big bunch of the less talented in the middle and some very old or very overweight stragglers. No-one quite understood how the scoring worked, no-one trusted the stopwatches of the race officials and sometimes no-one noticed some of the events were taking place at all. We turned up, sat around and chatted for a while, did our event and then went home.

Yet the league continues, and next year will celebrate its 113th birthday.

How does it work? How has it kept going so long?

'I'll tell you what,' said Mike, gasping after running a creditable twenty-four second hurdles for 8th, and last, place. 'I ain't been running with guys that quick since Strangeways in eighty-five. Jesus Christ, what are you trying to do to me you...'

It continues because of people like Mike, people like James and particularly people like Darren; competitors, athletes, every last one of them.

'If that leg ain't better by next week Darren, I'm going to buy you one down at Blackbush market.'.

Darren looked back at him, then hobbled down the straight. 'I'm going to see if I can stretch to the relay,' he yelled. 'It might have cleared up by then.'

After the first meet of the season, our club is sitting in second to last place in the league, after Blackheath's minibus broke down on the way to the venue. A proud history is set to continue.

Now Dwayne has passed, and I am left back in fourth place. Cornelius and Patrick are disappearing up the towpath and I have nothing left to respond with. It's time to stop. I need to consider who I am and what I am doing here, rather than about the race.

I think back to a conversation with my team captain, after my last second-place finish.

'I feel shit Andy,' I said to him in the pub after the race. 'I've let you down, I'm sorry.'

Andy looked at a scrawled note of race stats and frowned. 'Of course you feel shit Evans. Look at these mile times – they're all over the place.'

'I know,' I said.

'Did you have a plan at the start of this race?'

'I was going to stay with the main pack for the first few miles, slowly pick up the pace and then use my momentum to carry me to the line. I presumed everyone else would be too tired to keep up.'

'Um, yes,' he said, looking back to the notes. 'But you haven't done that at all, have you?'

'No.'

'And now you have no momentum whatsoever.'

'No.'

He frowned and stroked his chin. 'What's your PB at this race again?'

'1.10.01.'

'1 hour ten…and one second?'

'Yes.'

'Could you not have found something extra at the end?'

Back in the race Cornelius, Dwayne and Patrick have stretched further into the lead.

'Nothing,' I said.

'Really?'

'Yes.'

He knew why. He knew that I was scared of pushing it too far. 'Well perhaps you should start running at exactly one hour-ten pace. Five-ten a mile, and a not a second slower. Then try and improve it by one second for the last three miles. The memory of missing seventy minutes by one second, should be enough to push you on.' He looked back to the lap times and shook his head. 'And stop thinking about everyone else in the race. They're just ghosts. Nothing they can do will hurt you.'

Cornelius, Dwayne and Patrick bunch into a group. They're working off each other, trying make it easier for them to escape together.

Andy was right as always. Running is simpler alone. I know how fast I can go, so I need to run at that pace and then slowly try to push myself a little bit quicker. I won't like it, but my body will obey. It is only thoughts that slow me down.

My thoughts are a ghost in the past.

The course swings onto a residential estate. People stand outside their houses clapping politely. There is a church on one side and a school on the other. At the gates, pupils play musical instruments to try and encourage the runners – trumpets, clarinets, cymbals. I recognize the song:

Dur de de dur de de dur durr. De de de durr de de de durrr.

It's the theme to Wallace and Gromit.

Dur de de dur de de dur durr. De de de durr de de de durrr.

Instead of thinking about the race, I start to sing along in my head

Dur de de dur de de dur durr. De de de durr de de de durrr.

And my pace increases.

Dur de de dur de de dur durr. De de de durr de de de durrr.

And again.

Dur de de dur de de dur durr. De de de durr de de de durrr.

And again.

Dur de de dur de de dur durr. De de de durr de de de durrr.

Soon I'm up to five-minute mile pace, and while the song stays in my head, it doesn't seem to feel hard.

Dur de de dur de de dur durr. De de de durr de de de durrr.

No other thoughts matter now. My mind is empty and my body is free to move.

I catch Fabien, then we run together towards the mile marker. There's a water stop at the side of the road. Patrick, Dwayne and Cornelius take a drink and race off together, but I don't need to. They think they're thirsty and they are weaker because of it. I'm not thinking. I'm strong.

Mile end. 5.14. Fourth place and catching.

MILE 10

The parps and clangs of the school band fade, and the route ascends towards Richmond Park and the main road back towards the finish. It's not much of a hill, maybe a hundred meters, but it is enough to test the energy of the group of three ahead of us. I don't even think about them as I drive up the concrete.

I'm not interested in you. I'm running for myself. It is just a hard training session – me and the hill – and nothing else. I am faster and I'm not even thinking about it. Dur de de dur...

Patrick has bolted to ten or twenty meters ahead, still accelerating to the top of the hill, but Dwayne and Cornelius are slowing on the way up, while Fabien is still going alongside me, calm and collected as usual.

The ten-mile barrier should be a good point for the road runner – it is the threshold at which you can begin to release the energy you've been conserving for the end – however for Dwayne and Cornelius it is a warning sign. They're taking repeated sips of water before discarding their cups on the side of the road. They're tired. Three miles to go, still a long way. Fifteen more minutes of pounding. Fifteen more minutes of pain. It might not seem like much, but when there is nothing left in your legs and your lungs, it can be a long, long way.

As I drive to the top of the hill, I try to use my arms instead of my legs. This way the road will not seem as steep.

Faster and faster. The top is almost there. Keep pushing and keep rotating. You are the road runner, you are the road runner, run run run run run. Ruun run-run ruun, run run run run. And….breathe. And breathe again.

As long as I can grab hold of the earth and pull myself up, I can make it to the top.

Patrick is almost at the summit, while Cornelius and Dwayne toil, slipping back with every metre. I run alongside Fabien, and then we catch them with a few metres of the hill left to go. I want to look over at their sweating faces, but instead I accelerate past, inching ahead of Fabien as I go.

Patrick is at the top and is turning onto the main road. I focus on his gangly physique, repeating the Wallace and Gromit song in my head and imagining myself at end of a Looney Tunes sketch – Wile E Coyote chasing after the Road Runner. I run with renewed vigor, repeating the tune in my head, and Fabien strides just behind, sweat blood-red on his shirt. We're damaged but not broken. Not yet.

Humm, hum hum. I am the road runner. I am the road runner. Humm, hum hummm.

We are at the top. I want to relax, but I can't. Things have changed. The new Ben doesn't slow down at the top – he accelerates. Losers slow down, and I am not a loser anymore.

Patrick doesn't concern me much. If he keeps going as he is, with his flailing limbs and gasping breaths, then there is no way I am going to catch him. You cannot race a madman. I just have to let him do his thing and if he beats me, then so be it. However, I need to make sure that I pull away from Fabien, and let Cornelius and Dwayne drop back as far as possible. They all have fast finishes, and while they can still see me, they can still win.

Fabien takes a deep breath, then coughs. His style has become ragged again. It's as if he's still running up the hill.

Patrick is a cartoon figure ahead, dashing down the road back to Richmond. He is the Tasmanian Devil, whirling his limbs in a tornado, and I must catch him before he spins out of control.

Wait a second.

He has.

He has spun out of control.

I'm running straight past him.

What's happened?

By a tree on the side of the road he lays prostrate, his red vest flung onto the ground. I can hear him groan in frustration. He knows there is no point in carrying on. Patrick Owosu is out of the race.

The Runner's Journal Entry 10 – Injury

As a runner I have a funny conception of pain. While a normal human being will understand it in a sane, rational way, for instance:

If I cut my hand with a knife it will hurt.
Because it hurts I will stop cutting my hand.
I will try not to cut my hand with a knife.

…A runner welcomes it.

If I run really fast it will hurt.
I want to run really fast to get quicker.
I want to run so it hurts.

Pain is a part of running. It is the yardstick by which we judge our improvement. It is not something to be avoided but something to strive for and embrace.

However, every so often there will come a point where we are reminded what pain is like for everyone else. It is when injury strikes.

A regular supply of endorphins means that runners have a feeling of invincibility about them, but ironically this makes them very susceptible to injury. Run too much, too quickly, too hard – feel too invincible – and the muscles will become as fragile as a new-born baby's skull. Run again after this and they will break.

'Ow.'

'Ow.'

'Ow...shit, ow.'

It's the worst feeling a runner can have, and the moment we fear above all others. That's why when it happens, we're not very good at dealing with it.

Stage 1 – Denial

'What? What's wrong with you?' you say to yourself. 'Come on, keep going, it will disappear in a minute. You'll run it off.'

But it doesn't. It hurts again and again, and the denial level increases accordingly.

'Come on! Jesus, you're a wimp. Go, away! It's all in the mind. Let it go, it's all in the mind.'

But it stays. And the pain gets worse and worse, and worse.

'I can't. I can't keep going. I've got to...I've got to stop.'

Then it hits you.

'I'm injured. I'm actually bloody injured.'

And you feel very, very human.

Stage 2 – Blame.

'That crack in the pavement;

  These bloody trainers;

  The wrong energy drink;

  A change in the weather;

  God looking down and cursing me.'

How could it happen to you? How could you – decent, hardworking, diligent runner you – get injured? What did you do to deserve it?

You get angry because it is not your fault. The injury has been caused by something outside of your control and, unless you have been assaulted with a spanner, it is something that you are unable to vindicate. You have to resign yourself to fate:

'I'm injured and there's nothing I can do about it. I'm pathetic. I'm pathetic and I cannot run.'

Which is when the next part of the process arrives.

Stage 3 – Melodrama.

Most runners are very strict on themselves. They have a specific training schedule that they have to keep to, and if it changes they become very neurotic:

'If I don't do at least ten miles on Wednesday, I will lose ten minutes on my time.'

'I have worked so hard to get to this point. One week off and I will lose everything.'

'If I stop running I will become depressed, fat and want to kill myself. I must keep training.'

But now you don't have a choice, you cannot run. The nightmare has come true.

'That's it, my running career is over.'

'I'll never want to run again.'

'I don't want to eat, sleep or do anything. Life has no meaning anymore.'

One day into getting injured, I started to compare myself to a washed-up has-been – a footballer drinking himself to death, a swimmer who could not stop eating, a boxer with no brain cells left. So much had I put myself on a running pedestal, that I had convinced myself I had fallen off for good:

'My life! What should I do with my life? Will I ever find anything else?'

I did find something else – TV, chess, the ukulele – but none of it compared to running.

The feeling carried on for a week or two. Eventually I got over it, but in my heart and hearts I still wanted to run. Then I came towards the final stage.

Stage 4 – Convalescence.

After endless welling in depression and anger, an amazing set of revelations come upon you. Injuries heal! Sitting and doing nothing helps. Your body can make itself better.

This might seem an obvious conclusion to the normal person, but to a runner it is quite the epiphany. For us, the body is a blank canvas, and the act of running the paintbrush. Only by running will there be any colour to our world.

Run. Get fitter. Then run again.

But during injury, your body manages to improve itself without running. It goes against everything you've convinced yourself to be true, but it works. Your leg starts to feel stronger. If anything, it feels better than it did before.

Finally, now everything is better, you are able to accept the truth. Rest works. Injuries heal. You can run again, and you can probably run about as quick as you did before.

'My leg is fine.

My body has healed itself.

I can beat injury.

I can beat any injury in the world!'

And once again you are invincible.

Then it begins to hurt again and you need another week to recover, but that's okay now. You will get better. Being injured is not the end. Pain has been overcome.

I look at Patrick and open my arms in a hopeless gesture. I presume he must have pulled a muscle or picked up a stitch, or simply burned out – I don't know, it could be so many things. I try to tell him that I want to help, that I would stop if I could and that I am not a bad person for keeping going.

He responds with a faint nod. He understands. He is a racer. He knows that whatever happens, whatever anyone else is feeling, we have to keep going.

When I think about his pain, I feel the muscles in my leg contract, and I wonder how close I am to a similar fate. Will I be too tired to do anything about it? Will I be able to push on?

Fuck it, its pain and it hurts, but so what? I can't do anything about it. All I can do is endure and hope that it doesn't get any worse, and if it does, I'll just endure it even harder.

We all feel this at some point in our lives. Work, family, friends, money, getting out of bed in the morning – in a way it's all one great endurance test. If we choose life and everything that comes with it, then at times it is going to be hard. Running is the same – it's just that in running the difficulties are much more straightforward. Pain, then fatigue and then endurance. Pain, fatigue and endurance. Pain, fatigue and endurance. Simple. Life is far more complicated.

Fabien coughs again, and I push forward, opening up a metre gap. Endorphins rush through my body. Through all the madness and the hurt, as we head into Richmond with just over two miles to go, I am ahead. If I can keep going now with one last effort, I can win. Just over two miles – anyone can run that far. I am tired, but I still have something left. Of course I do, I am Ben Evans.

I am the road runner.

4.59 – floating on air.

MILE 11

Fabien begins to drop behind. His fluid style has become ragged and his breaths are loud and laboured. I run diagonally over the road to make sure he can't follow me, then increase the pace for a few seconds to increase the gap. The effort is intense, but I know I can keep it up. I won't get another chance to drop the Surrey champion, so I need to make every effort count.

My thighs burn.

His breaths still sound close behind.

Get away. Don't try and hang on. I won't let you touch me again.

Fabien appears again on the other side of the road. His long, fluid stride is back. I run diagonally to get alongside, and then up the pace once more. He follows for forty, fifty metres, then his breaths become heavy again and his strides shorten. As I ease slightly in front, he turns and looks at me, and shakes his head. Who are you? How can you run like this? What have you done with Ben, the man I always beat?

I don't look back. Slowly the sounds of his breaths disappear. I can't see him or feel him.

Get away. This is my race now. I don't want to hear you or feel you. Leave me alone for good.

He's gone. I want it more than him. I have beaten the Surrey champion. He won't come back now.

Blackness is the only thing in my head now. Infinite black.

Now pain. Pain and black.

Only myself, the road and the pain.

Nothing left.

There's a man stood on the roadside reading a newspaper. He has a black Labrador beside him, chewing on a stick. Neither of them seem to notice the race is taking place. I want to be like them. I want to idle away my Sunday morning. I want not to care. Why can't I be like them?

Pain in my legs, sickness in my stomach. Why did I have to push ahead of Fabien? What is good about this? Who makes this choice?

Look at the road. There is still so far to go.

Nothing is ever easy.

I can finish. I will finish, and it will be better. I'm at the front of the race, a special place. I need to stay here, need to keep pushing.

Nothing. No-thing. Don't think. Look down at the road – stare at the gravel, the broken glass, the tyre marks and the road and the road and the road…and think of nothing.

It's so hard being in front.

It feels okay. It feels…like sleep, calm, no-feeling, death.

Don't interrupt me. I want to stay this way.

My body is being stretched to its limits. It seemed so simple a mile ago, but now I'm in the lead, anything can go wrong. What happened? Why did this happen to me?

Sweat glistens off my skin and my leg muscles bulge like tumours.

Ugly. Weak.

A skeleton. Nothing left.

The Runner's Journal Entry 11 – The Body Beautiful

Last summer I was sat in the garden of my local pub. It was the first day of a heat wave and all the hunks and babes were shedding their winter cloaks and putting their tanned, shapely bodies on display. It was the moment they'd been waiting for. At some point a stranger's eyes would divert lustily in their direction and all the hard work they had put in over the winter months would be justified. They were attractive. People fancied them. It was all worthwhile!

I sat back in my seat and shuffled into the shade at the corner the table. I am one of the UK's top marathon runners. Over the same dark, winter months I have been working almost every muscle in my body, stretching it to its absolute limits, but no-one – not one person – takes a second look at me. They look at the guy opposite with the tight t-shirt and the toned biceps. Why? Because even though I exercise harder and longer than anyone else here, I am a runner and runners are not beautiful.

Running makes you incredibly fit. It is the best form of exercise to lose weight and use calories, but once the weight has gone, that's it. All the fuel has been spent pumping the blood to your legs; the rest of you – your arms, your chest and your face – is left scrawny and skeletal, a body starved of nourishment.

When I watched Game of Thrones the other night I didn't see any nine-stone men wielding swords, and the women had bulges in places other than their calf muscles.

No, running does not cause the opposite sex to flock your way when they catch a glimpse of your tight quads. Not at all.

So what's the point? Why do we engage so much of our time pursuing an activity which hinders our ability to attract the opposite sex? Isn't this against our evolutionary code?

As the next girl walks past me and heads to the bouncer in his tight t-shirt, I wonder if I should take up a different sport, like rowing or weight-lifting. But then I remember something. I am not one of them. I do not make all this daily effort for the sole purpose of looking good in a nightclub. I am more interesting. It takes more to satisfy me than a wink from the town hotty.

Yes Dr Freud, I know, it probably is all about sex at the end of the day, but my understanding of sexuality is different. I want people to fancy me because I have achieved things, because I have commitment, stamina, guts and enthusiasm, not because my body bulges out of a tight pair of jeans. I am the anonymous artist, the brooding rock star, the beautiful actor who picks ugly roles. Running doesn't make me better looking, but I like to think it makes me an attractive person, and if people can't see this then they are not people I want to be with.

When I look at the bouncer, standing by the door with a beautiful girl on his arm, I consider what it took for him to become this way. He must have spent hours and hours pumping the muscles in his arms until his mind stopped working. This is anaerobic fitness. That's how it works. If you do it right and do it well, you should not be able to think. The exercise turns you into an amoeba.

Being a long-distance runner is different. Reaching optimum pace engenders another feeling altogether — a Zen state — where you become one with the world around you, where your legs move with nature and your muscles, joints and heart *all work in harmony. Bodybuilders are doing something similar, but they can never open the door long enough to see what the runner can – the weights will always have to be dropped to the floor before their consciousness can appreciate what is around them.*

So, as I sit in the shady corner of the pub sipping my lemonade, I realise that I may not be beautiful and no-one will look at me when they walk to the bar, but I know I have inner beauty that most other people can only dream of. Look long enough and you will see it too.

Enjoy the hot weather beautiful people. My light shines from the inside.

At the side of the road is Ham village green. Well-dressed families walk across it to church, slow, smart and measured. Only the dogs run. Dogs and me.

The road is busy. Cars, buses and cyclists. Occasionally supporters cheer me on. The freak. I'm the freak.

The sky – a blue haze. The sun – a snarling light. Concrete smashes my legs into a pulp.

The machine. I am a machine that never stops. I am a car with no driver. I'm not like them. I am the road runner.

I haven't seen anyone since Fabien dropped back and I wonder if something has happened. Maybe they stopped to help Patrick? Maybe they're coming back to hunt me down. I am the bad man, the one who didn't stop.

I doubt it. I definitely doubt it, but I don't want to look round to check. I don't want to think about them, because it will only make me feel paranoid about being ahead, and I don't want to feel anything.

I check my watch. Only two minutes gone. What's that – not even half a mile? Not even close. Oh God, oh God.

Run quicker and you will be finished quicker.

Pain is failure leaving the body.

I can't think about the finish, because it makes the moment so much worse. I can't think about pain, because pain would mean feeling, and I cannot feel.

Thus shall ye think of all this a fleeting world.

A star at dawn, a bubble in a stream.

A flash of lightening in a summer cloud.

A flickering lamp, a phantom, a dream.

Nothing is permanent. I am merely a succession of different thoughts. Life is a journey and the race is just part of it. Each step is one thing, and then something else after that. It isn't better or worse.

I am now, this mile, this road, this Ben, and soon I will be something else. What experience. What intensity. What a world this is. My world.

Another minute gone, leaving only one and a half to go. The road is approaching Ham village on the edge of Richmond Park. Not far to the finish.

Don't think. Don't think – run. Think when the mile is over.

A house now. Then a winding road. Another house, then up and down over a little bridge. A pub and a stream and a family on bikes. This way. Keep going. Not far to go now.

Another turn in the road. A house. A shop and then another house. The house is making noises. The red front door has a mouth – breathing in, breathing out, coughing and spitting. Over the windows is a black and white vest. A black and white vest. An orange vest and a blue Mohican. Tanned walls. Muscles. An orange and Bermuda shorts. A blue Mohican.

Don't look over. Don't think about them. I am what I am. There is no-one else.

Mile over. They can't have caught me. I'm the road runner.

5.00 dead. Dead.

MILE 12

Dwayne Barratt. Cornelius Cooper. Ben Evans.

Orange vest. Black and white vest. Green vest.

Blue Mohican. Blond thatch. Thinning mess.

PB 1.08. PB 1.12. PB 1.10

Three half marathon wins. Two half marathon wins. Zero half marathon wins.

Nutcase. Workaholic. Loser.

Only one of us will win

There are 2.1 miles to go. We've been running for fifty-eight minutes. The path has led us along the Thames, through Kingston and back into Ham village for a finish in the local park. It is time for someone to take a lead, but none of us want to. Five minutes a mile is good enough for all of us. It keeps us where we are, and guarantees a top three finish, without more hurt and fatigue.

No-one wants to kick too early and then be caught with a hundred metres to go. That would be more painful than anything. But at the same time, none of us want to lose in a sprint for the line. That would mean all our hard work coming to nothing.

None of us want to do anything. For a second I wonder if we should be racing at all.

The Runner's Journal Entry 12 – A Small Victory

This is why we do it right? This is why we run over and over, day after day, rain wind or shine. This is what it all builds up to – the fastest, the strongest, the toughest...the winner.

I've done it. I've done what I set out to do. I am validated as a human being.

This is how it feels when you cross the line. The fact that you have beaten 'him' or 'her' is of no importance, but the fact that you have beaten your doubts, your worries and the constant uncertainty, is the ultimate triumph. Of course, there are numerous facets to running that make you feel good – the relaxation, the sense of achievement, the endorphins – and all are good enough reasons to do it on their own, but none of them give you the same sense of definitive, unequivocal justification as winning. It is the culmination of all the hard miles. It justifies all that came before.

The problem is that feeling is ephemeral. It only lasts for a few minutes. Then the emptiness creeps in.

What now? What's next on the journey? Where's the next mountain to climb?

Human nature doesn't cope well with satisfaction. We're transient beings, not ones to rest on our laurels. Even some Olympic champions find it hard to cope after the games have finished. They've done everything there is to do, where do they go now? Athletes are the modern equivalent of Sisyphus pushing the boulder up the mountain. They are happy when they get to the top, but they are even happier when the boulder falls back down the hill and they have to start all over again. They can keep doing what they love doing. They can keep running.

In the same way most writers don't write to become published authors, and musicians don't write songs to become pop stars – athletes don't run to win. They like running. They want to become as good at it as they can. They enjoy going out on a rainy Sunday morning and running sixteen miles faster than they ever have before. They like racing, because in races they can run faster than in training, and if they win, then great. It's a nice feeling and they're not going to complain about it, but it's extraneous to the overall purpose. Think of it like Christmas Day. we don't ask for it, we don't base the other 364 days of the year around it, but it's a nice day all the same.

However, that's not to say that winning doesn't have a purpose. It still validates what athletes do. I think of it as a bit like getting married. It doesn't make you really feel any different and it's not a patch on the feelings that put you there in the first place, but somehow it justifies it all, making your love for another person something real.

This is what I feel on the podium after the race. Scores of people look at me and clap when I receive my trophy, and even though I smile and waved sheepishly back, I'm not celebrating myself. Rather I'm celebrating the joy that comes with running, and how great it makes you feel whether you're first, second or fifty-third. I know this, runners know this, but sometimes you need to show it to everyone else, to validate what it means. Try as I might, convincing a non-runner that running sixteen miles on a freezing Sunday morning is a wonderful experience, is almost impossible. Only in winning can I show them that joy.

I wave again to the crowd again.

I love being a runner. I love running and what it means to me, and if I can validate this love and show it to the rest of the world, then winning does have a meaning, and that's good enough for me.

THE ROAD RUNNER

Two miles to go. I've been here many times before. It's the nadir, where energy is at its lowest and where muscles are starting to eat themselves alive. You know you will finish, you know that you have done okay to get to where you are, you know that it has been an achievement getting to this position and there would be no shame in staying where you are, but…but you can't. That isn't good enough. You want to be a top runner, one who doesn't let up until they've crossed the line. You didn't get here by accepting the simple way out. You want to do better. You want to win. That's why the voices echo in your head:

It's not far to go.

Do I feel alright?

How do they feel?

Have I got it?

Can I sprint away?

Is it too early?

Where's Fabien?

Do I really want to win this?

Am I even a winner?

What is it going to take?

Have I got it in me?'

How much do I want it?

I have good reason to feel unsure. I have a reputation as a running loser. From when I first took up the sport, it has stuck to me like the remnants of a blood blister. I am the nearly-man, the one who tried hard, the one who could have almost done it, had it not been for... (insert excuse here).

It all started when I finished 522nd in the Reading Half. 522nd, in my first half marathon! 522nd out of 12,000 people! I must have been a natural. Two or three months and I'd be on top of the podium.

I entered my next race – the Clandon Park 10k in leafy Surrey, feeling sure I would win. It was a local affair in the grounds of a stately home and the competition mostly looked like they were there for a Sunday stroll. A victory was all but assured.

At the start I sweated with expectancy, visualizing the finish line and the glow of success that would come over me as I crossed it. It took less than a mile for me to realise I was out of my depth. For five minutes I ran like a maniac, huffing and puffing, desperately trying to hang on to first place, then second, then third, while the guy in front, a thirty-minute 10k runner, strode relentlessly on ahead. I had no hope and I was feeling very sick. The next five miles were torture. The course undulated through long grass and muddy ditches, and climbed up to a steep hill at the end. I came in eighth. Winning and running were not as easy as I thought.

Not to be deterred, I took three months out to train properly. My pride was dented but my ambitions remained. I worked over and over, lowering my times at the local parkrun by minutes, motivated by the failure of my last race. Then I returned for another 10k, the unimpressive sounding 'Samaritans Run' in Crowthorne.

One mile in, I realized I was much fitter than before. I was running just metres behind first place and the exertion was nothing like I'd felt a few months before. I was there, with the leading bunch. It was only a matter of time before I could make my move.

The course was a two-lap maze through the grounds of a Berkshire school, finishing with a lap of the playing fields. With four hundred metres to go I was in first. Just one more lap of the field and I would make it – I would win! My running career would be off into orbit. So which way did I go? Left or right? The finish was over there so.... well, we went round the field the first time so...

I was still running three minutes later.

'Where's the finish?' I yelled to a marshall.

'Oh, you've got one more lap to go yet,' she replied kindly.

'I've done fucking two!' I said.

She pointed back to the line a hundred metres behind me, where cheers were ringing out for Steven Bailey as he sprinted in for victory. 'You must have taken the wrong turn love.'

In the five years since this day, I have taken three more wrong turns, set off too fast twice and been beaten by better racers hundreds of times. Once I was overtaken by Fabien with ten metres to go, and another time I was waving to the crowd when Cornelius came from nowhere and sprinted past for victory. However most of the time I have simply lost because I am not good enough. I'm not a winner.

Unless you are the Olympic Champion, what is winning to the runner anyway? It only says one thing – the race you are in is not hard enough. The whole point of racing is to make you a faster runner, not for glory, not so you can beat another five hundred guys.

Running is all about the journey, and the journey must be one of development and improvement, otherwise there is no point. If you're not striving to be all can you be, then you might as well sit at home and watch Chariots of Fire, because you have achieved nothing. Second is everywhere, first is nowhere – that's what I tell myself. For my whole running career, I have been improving. I still want to win though, just once. Am I now ready to take the next step?

We rejoin the side of the river, meaning it is now a straight race along to the Thames to the finish in Ham village park.

Cornelius begins to make a move.

I stick on his back like limpet, stubbornly refusing to lose even a millisecond of pace. This isn't tactical. It is simply because I don't like him, that today he will not be the winner, and for a couple of minutes it will give me the motivation to stay alongside. The pace hurts. 4.50 a mile I reckon, but I will get used to it. Surely he will not be able to keep this up?

Breathe.

Don't think, don't think, don't think.

Breathe.

Don't think, don't think, don't think.

Breathe.

I stare at Cornelius's Wimbledon vest – black and white, black and white, black-white, black-white – and try and let it relax my mind. Follow him, follow him. It's simple. Follow. Black and white, black and white.

A gust of wind comes over the river and pitches me a few inches off the path. I panic for a moment. What's happening? Is my energy going? Have my legs given up? I see colours – green, blue and red – and feel like I'm going to faint. I can't do it. I can't keep up. It doesn't matter, I don't need to win.

My brain switches back into focus. What a wimp. Come on, fucking come on! You have shown how strong you are. Remember how hard it was when you started, when running a mile felt like death, and your legs felt like they'd been hit with a sledgehammer? Think about how far you have come – to those times when you trained so hard you couldn't walk, when you somehow managed that last quick mile after a long run, when you sprinted to the top of the hill just before vomiting. Think about what you can do now, compared to the weak individual you were.

Look at the river, the grass and the great city beyond.

Dwayne passes me on the right.

Think about the sublime – the great expanse of nature, the great expanse of your mind.

Think about what we are capable of as human beings.

It's not about winning or losing. It's about realizing who you can be. Now is the time to find that out, to see just how far you can go.

I match Dwayne's stride.

The mile is almost up. The bridge is up ahead and there are crowds of people lining the street. They are looking at you. They wish they could be the person you have become.

Don't miss this chance. Don't give up now.

We pass Cornelius.

It's not a race or a contest. It's a journey through life. You have to take another step, no matter how much it hurts, because otherwise you will fall down and have to start all over again.

Now there are two, Dwayne and me. Cornelius is broken. He has reached his limit and we have gone further. He cannot look within, because he doesn't know what it means to suffer like this. He can only see the black road.

I can see more than this, and so can Dwayne. We both can. The last mile will be ours.

Mile 12 – 4.55. Time is irrelevant now.

MILE 13

The towpath merges onto the road. It is a clear, concrete mile to Ham village park. Only one mile to go – anyone can run that far.

If I was in sixth or seventh, or seventeenth or ninety-sixth, I could make one last burst for the line and then leave happy with my day's work, but not this time. If anything causes me to fail now, I'll never live it down. If I don't find that last ounce of energy, that final burst of speed, then I will have failed, whatever I choose to tell myself or whatever other people say. For those back in seventeenth or ninety-fifth, it's okay. They don't need to go to this place. They will feel shattered at the end and they will want to vomit or pass out, but once they cross that line that will be enough for them. I know this because it's been good enough for me in the past. It's good enough for anyone who doesn't strive for more, who will never be a part of an elusive, exclusive winning club. I was one of them. I was always too weak and scared of making this choice, to push beyond pain and fatigue. Am I still one of them? Do I have the final push in me?

'Good luck mate,' says Dwayne, as we turn towards the park.

'Cheers,' I gasp, not wanting to say anything at all.

We increase the pace. I can barely open my eyes.

Dwayne knows what it takes to win. That's why he's so nice about it all. I like that he's nice because I don't want to hate him.

I start to tell myself that this isn't a race after all. I'm not here to compete. Competitors run on the track, around a short little oval, racing each other until they burn out, and that is not what we're doing. We are not racing. Running through the streets of Richmond, we are more like explorers crossing the desert. For us, it is the journey that's the challenge – the 13.1 miles of tarmac and towpath. It's not Dwayne Barratt or Cornelius Cooper, or first or second or third, it's completing the race in the fastest time you possibly can.

Dwayne pushes on ahead.

It does matter. I wasn't a competitor before, but I am now. Oh God, oh God, what am I going to do?

We are running faster than anyone in this race, I know that for certain. Although we are tired and well out of our comfort zones, our combined fear is enough to ensure that we will not be caught in the next 1500 metres. We shouldn't be able to run this fast, but in the circumstances we can.

This is why running is so complicated. We shouldn't be able to do what we are doing. I've never run this fast at the end of a half marathon in my life, but for some reason, with Dwayne just in front of me, I can do it. It's like suddenly being able to fly. You can't do it. You cannot get that far up in the air. You can't, you can't...but yet...somehow you can. You can and now you don't want to stop. You can fly, and you don't care what the reason is.

The race isn't about logic anymore. Winners are the ones able to fly.

I take the lead. I don't know why – it is much the harder thing to do in this situation – but I feel the need go it alone. Every time I look at Dwayne, at his tanned shoulders and his stupid, blue Mohawk, I feel frightened at what I have to do, however if he's not there and I can look inside myself, then it doesn't seem to matter so much. I can fly with freedom

The road turns and passes through a parade of shops. I can't see any signs or brands, only the facades dancing in a blur. I begin to float along the road, in perfect running flow.

It's better like this. I am away from the pain and the pressure. There aren't any winners or losers here. There's no-one shouting, no-one telling me what I should do, no-one saying over and over that I could be someone, that I could be a proper man, that I must push everything else away and run and run and run. In flow no-one tells you any of that. You can just run at your pace, allowed to be whoever you choose and let your legs float over the surface of the earth, going wherever you want to go.

I float towards a sign. There are words and voices shouting at me and they are getting closer and closer and closer…

Fuck. Stop talking. Let me stay in my flow. Don't make it hurt.

Noise. So much noise and pain, so much pain! Oh fuck, oh God, I can't breathe, I can't see. Shit, shit, shit.

Where is he? Where is he?

Don't look back. Don't look back – he's not ahead of you, you can see.

Don't look back, don't look back. Look at the sign, look at the road, look at how long to go.

The sign says Ham. Ham village. Twenty kilometers in. One more turn and then into the park. Long straight road, then the finish. That's all.

Shit, shit, shit. I'm winning. I can't be. I don't want to.

Gasp, gasp, gasp.

Gasp, gasp, gasp.

I don't have the energy. No blood, no oxygen.

Gasp.

Is it now? Is it now? Is this the last straight?

Gasp, gasp, gasp.

No, I'm still here. It's still there. The road is still there.

Gasp, gasp, gasp…breeaathhhe.

Faint, faint, going to faint. Don't want to faint.

Keep thinking of flow. That's where you go when you feel like this.

You want to hurt, you want the fatigue. Keep the feeling going and let it grow like a rose. I love feeling tired. Let it bloom. Smell it. Let the pain become you.

Gasp, gasp, oh God.

Gasp. Gasp. Gasp.

The park. The park and a marshall. Is it? Is it?

'Where...?' I pant, as she points towards the final straight. 'Am...I...?'

I run past before she can answer. Is he there? I don't know.

It is a long straight road all the way to the park, and it's empty. No people now. No cars or shops. One long road. One long road, Dwayne and me, and then the end.

'This way!' I hear the marshall say as Dwayne passes her. 'Only half a mile to go now.'

Half a mile. That's eight hundred metres. Only two laps of a stupid, little track. I have about a five-second lead.

I let out a smile. That was the worst fatigue I will feel, and I have managed to get through it. Eight hundred metres and then I can return to the world. Normal breathing, movement without pain, thought without fatigue. I'll be able to stand or sit, or lie on the ground; hug, kiss, talk; exist with others, exist in the world; laugh...love!

I love being the road runner. Sometimes it can be calming and peaceful, and sometimes it can be more painful than it is possible to imagine, but it always reminds that there is good in the world – at the end.

What a place that will be. The moment I cross the line I am going to cherish it forever.

Twenty more seconds. I must be almost there. There are people gathered at the corner of the road looking expectantly. They are looking at me, looking and staring and shouting, ready to cheer and welcome me over the line. Their faces are getting closer and closer. Their eyes stare and their mouths open…but they are not cheering or clapping. They are looking.

I realize it isn't me they are looking at. It is something beside me, something next to my right arm. A silhouette – orange vest and blue…blue spike of hair – coming up beside me. Seven hundred metres to go. Seven hundred metres to the line. He's going to pass me. I am going to lose it. How? Why? Why now? Why have I done this?

There is a foul thunder of breath and thuds, and then a flash of orange. I am covered by a wave of pumping veins and wild, thrashing arms. It's the devil. The devil has come alongside, to drag me into his awful world – orange and blue, pain…and hell.

Dwayne strides one metre ahead, then two, then three, and I let him go. All I want is the comfort of the line. I don't want to win anymore. I don't want to run. I want to lie down and love the world that I miss so much, which I had forgotten amongst the training and battling, which is a good place after all.

For one small, pathetic moment I think this. Then I return.

I

WILL

NOT

BE

BEATEN

LIKE THIS

NOT HERE

NOT NOW

NOT BY YOU

NOT TODAY!

NOT BY YOU

NOT TODAY!

I close my eyes and run as fast as I can.

I can't see, I can't think and I can't feel. I plummet to the bottom, and then fall further, through heaven and hell, into my lungs and my stomach and out through my bowels, to a place where there are no thoughts or feelings or body or soul, where we can't think or see or touch, where pain is meaningless and tiredness forgotten.

Black. Black everywhere.

I don't want to be here, but it's the only place where I can find the energy to keep going. I have to stay with him. It's that or failure, which is worse than anything.

I open my eyes. Dwayne is only a metre ahead. I sprint into his wake and then pass him on the turn into the park. A crowd of people stand around two columns, within sight. There's a sign above them. Finish. I can see it.

Dwayne pushes back beside me.

There are still four hundred metres to go, and four hundred metres is a long way. I can't think about the finish yet.

I close my eyes and sprint again. I don't think about who these people are, or where the finish is. I just run as fast as I can.

You cannot sprint all the way, no matter how quick you are, but I'm going to, I am not going to let up. I am going to sprint the full four hundred metres, because for another minute and ten seconds I am not bound by human rules. I've been dreaming about this moment for the last five years, and I'm not letting that slip away now. I don't want to wake up.

Dwayne is still right behind me. I can feel his large biceps cutting through the air, pushing me harder and harder, pounding into my legs and my stomach, hitting me again and again and again and again. With every second my focus fades…

Trees

Flowers

Clouds

Happiness

Finish

Rest

I squeeze my eyes tight.

Harder

Harder

Keep pushing.

Harder, hurt, pain, anger, black, black, black, black, black...

Black

Finish.

Five hundred men and women put their hands on their knees and gasp for air

Five hundred men and women look at their watches

Five hundred men and women shake hands and pat each other on the back

Five hundred men and women suck on drinks and bite bananas

Five hundred men and women lie and look at the sky

Five hundred men and women put on foil and coats, jumpers and hats

Five hundred men and women are happy, all at the same time

Five hundred men and women love the world and everything in it

Five hundred men and women never want to do this again

Five hundred men and women will be back next year

It's not about winning or losing, or coming first or second or four-hundred-and-ninety-second. That's not what the road race is. It's about this, about this feeling – the collective glow of achievement, of a hundred warm bodies embracing at one time. It's finding parts of ourselves that we've never known before. It's knowing that an hour or two ago we were scared and wished we'd never signed up in the first place, but that we'd survived and we'd succeeded, and that we'd been better than we ever could have believed. Yes it's been hard, yes it's been long, but that is why it feels so fantastic now.

Soon we'll all be back to normal, the endorphins will have faded, and we'll get in the car and drive home, but for the next hour the feeling will be nothing but elation.

Remember mile eight?

That last straight towards the park?

The long stretch into Kingston?

Oh, it was awesome.

I went too fast at the start

I was too slow in the middle

I followed the wrong group

I didn't follow anyone

I still fucking did it though!

The moment I cross the finish line I don't look at the crowd, I don't look at the time and I don't look if I have won or lost. I look at Dwayne. I look directly into his eyes and tell him what a great race I think he's run. He looks back and winks. Neither of us can say much, but neither of us need to. When you share an experience like this, you create a bond that doesn't require words. We'll remember it forever.

Cornelius crosses the line in third, with Fabien coming a minute or so behind in fourth. I congratulate both of them, and they pat me on the back and tell me how well I raced, and how happy they are that I've won. I know they mean it too. I know, because I have felt the same way about them when they have been the victor and received the accolades. There is no animosity, no sense of being cheated or let down. It was all down to the best person on the day – the road runner – the one with the fittest body, the strongest mind and the purest soul.

Today my body was in great shape. I had trained harder, eaten better and kept a stricter routine than I ever had before. I had slept well and had felt calm at the start. I had stayed focused and kept going when the times were hard. Mentally I knew what I had to do, and I had achieved it.

But running is not just about this; it is about the soul as well. This is why it provides an experience greater than any other sport. For all of us who ran today – Cornelius, Patrick, Fabien, Dwayne and four hundred and ninety-five others – we all had to look to something beyond our bodies and our minds; at some point we had to stare into the depths of our soul, to find out who we were and who it was possible for us to be. Not all of us succeeded, but for a few seconds we had a glimpse, and could see the amazing person we had within us – a star twinkling, telling us that at the end of this there is something wonderful, something beyond the grind of day-to-day, something true and pure – something shining.

I will keep on running towards that light.

ABOUT THE AUTHOR

Ben is a writer, adventure cyclist and elite Marathon runner from Guildford in the UK. He completed his MFA at the University of Chichester, before quitting his job and cycling from Cairo to Cape Town. He currently holds the Guinness World Record for Marathon Dressed as a Dinosaur.

Printed in Poland
by Amazon Fulfillment
Poland Sp. z o.o., Wrocław